A MATCH MADE IN HATRED

MORGAN BRIDGES

A Match Made in Hatred — Dark & Dirty Vows
Book One
by Morgan Bridges

Copyright © 2021 Building Bridges Publishing

authormbridges@gmail.com

AUTHOR'S NOTE:

*D*ark romance is a genre that is a large spectrum of different tastes, kinks, violence, heat levels, and everything in between. Whatever your choice of entertainment, please note this book contains themes some readers might find uncomfortable. That is totally understandable and this book might not be for you. But for those of you who enjoy...forceful seduction, then welcome to the dark side.

EMILIA

*H*e's cloaked in a veil, born of darkness.

But if *veil* is changed to *evil*, is it not apropos? I would venture to say so. With the simple rearrangement of the letters, the meaning changes, becoming something more...

He's cloaked in evil, born of darkness.

Yes. Yes, this is much more fitting.

I know this on a deeper level than instinct can provide. Or maybe my senses have been sharpened by not utilizing them as a person normally would? Whatever the case, I know he's there, not more than ten feet from my bed.

His gaze roves over me, clinging to my body more than the blanket I'm under. A layer of fabric, or any shield, doesn't stop me from feeling his intense perusal, him studying me. I've often been watched, but this is different. Much more so.

As the daughter of someone who thrives in a world of crime, being looked at is nothing unusual for me. In fact, the cameras in the corners of my bedroom give my father's men ample opportunity to see me, and they do every day because I'm under surveillance.

For safety? Partially.

For compliance? Definitely.

However, this is always done through a lens, from another part of the mansion, not face-to-face. And most assuredly, it's never done alone with someone.

I've yet to open my eyes, and lift my lashes just a fraction to slide my gaze to the camera on my left. The red light that indicates it's operational is still on. At one point in my life, I despised that crimson circle, since it was a constant reminder of my captivity, but now I seek it out like a lifeline.

Where are my father's men and why aren't they here?

"No one will save you."

At the sound of the deep baritone voice, I turn my head and search for him. If I thought this man was a manifestation of my loneliness, or despondency, I now know that's not the case. His voice is nothing I'd conjure in my mind. It's too authoritative and arrogant, with a thread of mockery I find unpleasant.

The reassurance I gathered in my chest at the idea of being rescued by my father's men instantly dies. It morphs from a light emotion to one of heaviness; like a cannonball, it sinks to the bottom of my stomach, anchoring me to the mattress.

Are my father's men as dead as my hope?

If I'm killed, I'll be able to confirm here shortly when I meet them in the afterlife. And the murderer? He's the fallen angel from my childhood memories...

I squint into the darkness and try to make out the man's features. His hair is black, courtesy of the shadows, and his eyes are as well. That's if I remember correctly, but only the dawn can say otherwise, and I may not live to see it again.

He leans his tall frame against my desk and plants his hands on the surface behind him as if he has all the time in the world to linger. The act is casual, disarming, but I know better. Predators slink about as they circle their prey, keeping a short distance to create a false sense of security, and only their gazes show their true intent. It's a simple gleam that flashes in the eyes, right before their muscles tense and they attack.

I won't be taking my focus from his gaze. It might be the only warning I have.

"Sit up," he says. "I want to get a good look at you."

As if you haven't been staring at me this entire time.

The decision, of whether to obey, has my head throbbing. Normally, this wouldn't be an issue. My father has never shied from violence, and unfortunately that extends toward women, myself included. I quickly learned to do whatever he asked of me, because if he had to repeat himself…

It's not a lesson I needed more than once.

The stranger tilts his head just so. It's less than an inch, but it's enough. The energy in the room shifts, alerting me to my mistake. I'm scrambling into a sitting position before he pushes away from the desk and straightens. Even though he doesn't step toward me, his entire body is taut, as if he's prepared to strike at any moment.

I shove the midnight-blue curls from my face and tuck my legs underneath me. The moonlight that sneaks in through the window of my reading nook makes my nightgown appear white, but in reality it's a pastel pink. The square lacy collar stops just below my collarbones, and the hem bunches around my calves. I'm fully covered at all times because of being under constant watch, but right now it's not enough. The blanket didn't help either.

Vulnerability has me feeling naked and exposed while fully clothed. It's uncomfortable, to say the least.

The urge to wring my hands builds with the silence, so I place them in my lap and wait. As discreetly as possible, I flick my gaze over his face now that he's closer and I have a better view. A lock of hair has fallen over his brow, giving his disheveled appearance a devil-may-care look. Is that just a facade or does he wield enough power that breaking into my father's house doesn't faze him? His demeanor is that of a lord of the underworld, the unofficial title for the world of crime. This man's presence in my bedroom has to stem from something sinister.

His jaw and cheekbones have just the right angles to give him a haughty countenance. And his slanted eyebrows, along with his collared button-down shirt open at the throat, complete the look. Once more I assess his gaze, and it almost shimmers with excitement.

It's not the prelude to an attack, but I can't dismiss it either.

I lower my gaze a little so he cannot see the worry that is sure to be there. Some people get off on the terror of others, so it's best not to tempt him. Whatever is holding him back from advancing is a barrier I don't want to disable.

"How quickly you defer to me," he says with a hint of surprise in his tone. "Are you a submissive?"

The words burn with shame when they form on my tongue and sweep past my lips. "I'm submissive."

At the feel of his fingers taking hold of my chin, I suck in a breath. I didn't hear him move, and it only confirms how deadly this man is. He roughly jerks my head up and brings my gaze to his. This time, I don't look away, in fear of what'll happen if I do.

He narrows his eyes, but they do not gleam. Not yet. "There's a big difference between being submissive and being *a* submissive." He turns my head to one side and then the other, and I don't fight him while he examines me.

I have no idea what he's searching for, but whatever it is, I hope he doesn't find it.

I've never thought of myself as a beautiful woman. If anyone were to ask for my evaluation, it would be that I'm pretty—nothing more, nothing less. However, attraction isn't necessary for someone to want to hurt you.

Another lesson courtesy of my father.

My heart rate, already chaotic with this man's proximity, races even faster. Anger is a feeling I buried deep long ago because it would only serve to put me in jeopardy. But I dredge it up, digging for and uncovering the strong emotion like a skeleton—something once dead and hidden away. It finally overrides the anxiety churning within me and spreads, heating my cheeks and causing my breaths to speed up, giving me life. I use it while it's still within my grasp.

"What do you want?" I ask, my voice soft but firm. "And who are you?"

As if I don't already know this man's identity. However, it's his intent that's missing. He lived in my subconscious for years until I finally laid the fantasy of him to rest, along with my desire for love. Yet here he is in the flesh, far from the hero I painted him to be. If the stories my father told me are anything to go by.

At the man's glare, I inwardly deflate but continue to meet his gaze. He releases my chin to slide his hand through the curls resting on the nape of my neck, weaving his fingers through them until he palms the back of my head. Once his grip is secure, he wrenches me forward, and I get fully on my knees to avoid falling. Although, I'm not sure I would in his strong hold. It brands like heated iron, searing me everywhere he touches.

Now he is closer than ever, and the scent of his cologne brushes my nose. I hate to admit it's like him: alluring and seductive. His breaths, unlike mine, are controlled and even, the warmth of them skimming my lips. I press them together to avoid the sensation again. It's more of a violation to my person than the hand gripping me. And the reason? There was a slight reaction, a tingling that has me wanting to experience it again.

Am I so starved for human contact that a mere exhale from his lips to mine has me yearning? Am I so lonely that his very touch makes me want to sigh with something that borders on pleasure?

"A moment of bravery?" He cocks his head. "If you don't recognize me as a threat, you are truly insane."

My insides clench at his mentioning my mental state. However, it's nothing I haven't heard before, and I'd be naive to think he never learned about that night at the gala, where I created a scene. It was memorable, to say the least.

Nerves combining with the need to remove the feel of his breath from my lips have me darting my tongue across them. His gaze zeroes in on the action and flashes. My entire body tenses in preparation for his attack. This signal has been lit, and it's blazing in his dark eyes, making them like newly polished onyx.

He doesn't give me time to respond. Instead, he uses the hand palming my head to delve further into my hair and fist it. The other he snakes around my waist, yanking me to him. I throw out my arms in a weak attempt to stop him, but my strength doesn't compare to his. Then I slam into his torso, and though it's hard like marble, it's warm. My breasts, belly, and palms are flush to his chest, and the contact, so close and intimate, has my senses overloaded.

I can't remember the last time I felt the touch of another person. I've been a prisoner in these four walls for so long that time has slipped from me, my mind's way of protecting me from really acknowledging how much of a solitary existence I lead. Not by choice, but that can't be helped.

So having this man's hands on me and his body pressed to mine? I'm in complete and total shock. I don't know what will make it worse: to close my eyes or not? If I do, will I absorb the sensation of touch more fully? Or will it prevent me from diving into a sea of panic? Already my breathing is erratic, making it difficult for me to inhale properly, and I swear my heart is about to burst from my chest.

With my eyes wider than the moon just outside and my lips parted, begging and searching for oxygen, I stare up at him when he speaks. His voice, like the rest of him, holds me prisoner.

"Tell me, little one, what will you do with that information, if I were to indulge you?" He cocks his head ever so slightly. "What could a madwoman do with knowing my name?"

"I'm not insane," I say. When he raises a sardonic brow, I all but force the words from my throat, finding it hard to concentrate long enough to gather my thoughts into a coherent sentence. Fortunately, my mind stores data, so all I do is let it roll off my tongue in a recital. "Fact: Less than 5 percent of the human population is diagnosed as insane, and given how you are acting, I'm inclined to think you fall into that minority."

He snaps my head back, using the hand that's fisted in my hair. The strands pull at my scalp, and I wince because of the pain, but I don't cry out. If he is truly crazed, then my suffering will entice him.

"You are either stupid," he says, his voice dangerously low, "or intelligent but obviously not enough to keep your mouth fucking shut."

I add his presumed threat to the rest of my problems. It's not because I don't care I'm in danger; it's more that I'm bewildered and cannot function appropriately. My body is waging war with my mind, and the effort to keep from leaning into him has me shaking. He may think the tremors are from fear, and he'd be right, though it's fear of my pull to him, not at the thought of him hurting me. Well, some of my trepidation comes from that, but it's being overrun. My mind is screaming at me to stay silent and not provoke him further, adding more stress to my already fractured logic. I know I shouldn't enjoy any of this, and a part of me doesn't, but it is overshadowed by the rest of me, which wants to experience more.

More conversation.

More contact.

More connection.

This man is tethering himself to me in minute ways he's probably not aware of. Each touch, no matter how cruel, and each word, no matter how harsh, is something I'm emotionally starved for. And this is despite my aversion to physical contact. Whatever brought him here is fueled by something ominous, maybe even sinister, but that doesn't stop what's happening to me. I blame the little girl who met him, the one who sees him from a different point of view.

Those rose-colored lenses will be shattered, given time. He runs in the same circles as my father, and he is despicable. Birds of a feather...

The man slides his hand from my lower back to grab my ass and presses my hips to his. This time I can't stop from gasping at the feel of his cock straining against my belly. It's harder than I thought one would be, but my research only explained so much. The internet is no substitute for personal experience.

He sways from side to side, rubbing his erection across my stomach as he says, "If you speak again, I will shove my cock between those pretty lips to ensure you shut the fuck up." His eyes more than gleam now, and my trembling grows stronger. He smirks down at me, obviously enjoying taunting me. "That way, the only sounds I'll hear are you gagging and swallowing as I fuck your mouth. And when I come, it will only be there because that's how you treat filthy whores whose fathers are fucking trash."

Maximus Silvestri is one of my father's enemies. It's no surprise to me because there are many, and now that I know what drives this stranger, it'll be easier to accept my fate; death, after a sequestered existence, waits for me. There are many things I will never do, things I will never see, and places I will never visit, but Maximus has given me something I'd never thought to experience.

The first bloom of arousal.

And like a red rose, it will be stained with the crimson of my innocence, my suffering, and ultimately my life.

MAXIMUS

*S*he is...

Words fucking fail me. Or perhaps there are too many at once?

Whore.

Insane.

Enemy.

Those are the ones that are loud and clear, feeding my hate and squeezing my mind like a vise. They've been swirling in my psyche, gaining momentum ever since my brothers and I first put our plans into motion. Revenge is a powerful motive and has been my obsession for so long that it's become like a lover to me, a fictitious wife who's always hovering and demanding attention. I've had to keep it at bay, restrained more securely than the women I fuck, or else my need for justice would cause me to behave rashly and without thought.

This is something I can't allow. Ever.

There is too much at stake.

I pride myself on many things, but my self-control is a main contender. Emotions are fickle things and cannot be relied on to make decisions. But to dole out violence? That's when I release them like a pack of wild dogs, letting them tear into their victim with relish.

If there were words for me, I'm sure they'd be just as inciting as the ones I've given this young woman shaking in my hold. What would Caruso's daughter think if she knew them?

Narcissist.

Killer.

Evil.

It doesn't bother me because they're true. Anyone who's been in my presence knows this instinctively. And based on the way the woman's staring at me, she senses this, knows what malignant words describe me. Just as I know the ones for her.

But there are others...

And they are opposing the first set, frustrating me to the point that the desire to kill her—in order to rid myself of this inconsistency and confusion—burns within my gut.

Enigmatic.

Courageous.

Alluring.

These are terms I never thought would surface to my subconscious when I entered her bedroom. I anticipated her hysterics and tears, followed by screaming and begging, but I received none of that. The daughter of a crime lord usually possesses an air about her often likened to a princess—a spoiled, manipulative bitch who will remain that way unless her father teaches her better.

Or her husband breaks her.

Instead, I've found a young woman who carries herself with more poise than a queen despite the fear lurking in her gaze. And like royalty, she articulates each and every word she speaks, giving me a notion of her education and intelligence.

Along with those things, she is brave and has looked me in the eyes when even grown men have been known to avert their gazes. I've been told depravity lives there, but if it does, then it's nothing I haven't seen my entire existence. And the darkness within me is nowhere to be found in her.

How do I reconcile this mysterious queen with the insane whore I expected to find? Simple. I will crush her, and whatever remains will be the truth.

With my hand on her ass and the other gripping her dark hair, I smirk down at her. "Is there anything else you wanted to say to me?" She shakes her head, and the action is minuscule because of my tight hold on her. "That is probably for the best, *donnaccia*."

I wait for a flicker of understanding to cross her face or for her green eyes to glow with anger at me calling her a whore, but there is no response. Either she doesn't speak Italian or *la donnaccia* is good at hiding her emotions.

But she won't be for long.

The saying goes, you can't squeeze blood from a stone. Well, I beg to differ. I'll squeeze until there's not a drop left.

And *la donnaccia* is clearly not made of granite. Her soft curves are molded to my chest, and they are much fuller and more rounded than her silhouette first led me to believe. The nightgown was no help either, but it's little more than a thin barrier and hardly one at that. I can feel every inch of her with great clarity, and my cock strains against the fabric of my pants. However, I don't allow lust to control me.

An erection is nothing more than a manifestation of physical attraction, and even in the semidarkness, I'm able to make out the delicate contours of her face, the gentle slants of her eyes, and the fullness of her lips. Yes, she is beautiful, maybe more than I anticipated.

But it changes nothing.

I slide my hand from around her back to snatch her jaw between my fingers in a bruising hold. "Remember what I said, *donnaccia*. Don't speak, not a single word." I loosen my grip to run my thumb across the seam of her lips in a subtle reminder of how'd I'd silence her with my cock, and their tiny quivers please me. Fuck, if she doesn't stop looking at me like this, I'll throw her onto the bed and ruin the vow I made: I'd rather jack off than stick my cock in the filth that's Caruso's whore of a daughter.

However, I'm not above using the threat of sex as a manipulation tactic.

"Come with me." I release her and step back from the bed, keeping my gaze on the young woman while she places her feet to the floor. "If you try to run, it'll only make things worse than they already are for you. Then again, I'm not sure they won't be more abysmal by the night's end."

I assume she's smart enough not to respond, and I turn on my heel before striding to the door. I'm not sure what's the best approach when it comes to her father, Alfonso Caruso. Would he be more enraged if she accepted her fate and submitted to me? Or would it pain him more to watch her fight me, knowing I will only subdue her by force?

Choices, choices.

All of them bring immense satisfaction, since they result in Caruso's suffering.

Her steps are light as she quietly pads behind me. Once we enter the long hallway, she stands to my right but not exactly by my side, as if she wants to stay out of my reach. Which is foolish because there's nowhere she is safe from me. If I can gain access to her in Caruso's heavily guarded house, then where else could she possibly hide?

Death is the only realm.

When we descend the staircase, I study her from my peripheral vision. With one hand, she grips the banister like it's going to keep her from drowning in the sea of evil that's filling her home, and with the other, she clenches the nightgown, keeping it from becoming tangled in her feet. The light from the mansion's office spills onto the marbled floor, enabling me to see her more clearly, and I'm surprised to find her attire a rosebud pink. The innocent color doesn't quite fit with the profile of her I've put together.

Another inconsistency that doesn't sit well with me.

Once we step onto the main floor, I take hold of her upper arm, and she flinches from the way my fingers dig into her skin, but she doesn't pull away or make a sound. *La donnaccia* may be insane, but perhaps even a lunatic can have a moment of lucidity if a threat larger than their mind comes about.

The entire office comes into view, displaying mahogany bookshelves that line the wall behind the imperial desk at which Caruso sits, his gaze narrowed and his face flushed. From alcohol or frustration, I wonder? To one side of him is the priest, Father Aldo, who is all but strangling the black beads of his rosary. He looks at me as if I am Lucifer in the flesh, although I've attended mass more often than not. He is the one who hears my confessions, and perhaps that is the reason he fears me. And then there is Dante, my most trusted enforcer. My brothers, Tristano and Rafael, would've loved to have been here, but it's not part of the plan, which extends beyond this night. We want Caruso to suffer slowly as his entire world falls apart, crumbling at his feet.

Starting with his whore of a daughter.

But I guess from this moment on, she'll be falling at my feet, where she fucking belongs.

"What the hell is going on?" Caruso shoots from his chair as we enter the room, and Dante slams both his massive palms onto the crime boss's shoulders and shoves him back down. The physical restraint may prevent Caruso from standing but not from speaking. "Why did you bring my daughter here?"

This isn't the exact moment of my revenge, but tormenting Caruso and Emilia will have to be enough for now. Death is too easy, too quick. Anyone who wrongs my family should be made to live in agony, so punishing this man over a long period of time is the only way. Maybe I can ask the devil for a special request once I send Caruso to hell to meet him. A good Catholic knows there is no good without evil.

"Good evening," I say. I position myself in front of the desk at which Caruso sits, keeping *la donnaccia* close. His gaze flickers between us, and I'm not sure what he's looking for, but he's quick to dismiss her. I don't let the confusion of that leak into my voice when I say, "Thank you for allowing me into your home and to finally meet...Emilia."

The woman jerks in my grasp when her name hits the air. I prolonged saying it so I could see her reaction in the light, and it's what I expected. She doesn't like the intimacy between us that it implies, and whether subconsciously or not, Emilia slightly pulls away from me.

In retaliation, I shove her almost completely in front of me, and she stumbles, but my hold on her arm keeps her upright. Then I anchor her to me by placing my other hand low on her quivering stomach, splaying my fingers so that the tip of my pinky rests just above her clit.

Every single thing I do, from the way I hold her to the words I speak, is with great intent. I want Caruso raging over the treatment of his daughter; this will have to keep my desire for blood at bay until the time comes.

He glares at the placement of my hand, his nostrils flaring. "What the hell is going on?" Caruso repeats. Although, this time he doesn't attempt to rise from his chair. Training him is easier than I thought it would be. That's a disappointment. "Why are you here, Silvestri?" he asks, his gaze roving over me once again. "Are you here to do your brother's bidding like the bitch you are? I know Tristano is the only Silvestri with enough balls to orchestrate something like this."

I smile, and Father Aldo swallows deep. "He didn't mean that, my son," the priest says to me, his gaze pleading. "Signor Caruso is distraught over his daughter being present, but no blood needs to be spilled. I pray I was not summoned to give last rites."

His final sentence comes out as more of a question than a statement, and I understand why. In the underworld there are more requests for funerals than there are for marriages. However, I'm not sure if the reason I brought him here will ease his worry or heighten it. If he values his life, he'll shut up and do my bidding until I dismiss him.

"My brother is quite busy," I say with a casual shrug, "but even if he weren't, this matter doesn't involve him. There can only be one groom after all." I laugh, and it's full of neither amusement nor joy; the sound is meant to compound the weight of my words, as well as emphasize that I'm the one with all the power. Which is true, because Caruso is far from laughter, and his olive complexion has paled considerably. Finally, the reaction I've been waiting for.

And Emilia's response to my announcement? She makes a choking noise like someone is strangling her, and that imagery causes my smile to linger for a moment more. Her entire body goes stiff against mine, and I delight in it. Terrorizing her is only a small reward, and it's mostly for her father's benefit.

Father Aldo makes the sign of the cross, while Caruso gapes at me, but Emilia has yet to move, perhaps even breathe. She better not faint and ruin this for me. Just to ensure that doesn't happen, I drag my fingers across the seam of her inner thighs, brushing the mound of her sex. That has her sucking in a much-needed breath right before her body shakes with tiny tremors that couldn't be felt if I weren't holding her so closely.

Her signature is not required to be on the marriage license because I have a number of police officers on my payroll, but I want to make this as horrific as possible for her father. And watching the devil incarnate take your daughter as a bride is the same as watching her be fucked and then sacrificed on an altar.

But worse, since death will not come for a long while yet.

"Yes," I say, my voice light and contradicting my dark intent. "Today I will take Emilia to be my lawfully wedded wife, and you are to bear witness. That's why you are here, Father," I say, glancing at the priest. "There will be no need for last rites unless Caruso dies from natural causes in the next ten minutes. With that being said, we wish to be married. *Now*."

EMILIA

$\mathcal{M}$y heart is racing so quickly I cannot distinguish one beat from the next. They are just one continuous rhythm, a thrumming that all but drowns out every sound around me. The loud hum fills my ears and distorts my mind, making it difficult for me to process the events happening right before my eyes.

My father sits with his entire brow wrinkled and his eyes gaunt. Maximus's enforcer stares at him with one hand palming the weapon at his side, an expression of anticipation on his face. Meanwhile, the priest crosses himself so much that his hand is a blur, and he's switching among English, Italian, and Latin in his prayers. These are the things directly in front of me, offering a visual that should be clear, but it fades.

And Silvestri becomes my sole focus.

His breaths fill my ears, and the warmth of them heats the side of my neck. Everywhere he touches me is burning as though he's fire and I'm ice. My body even shakes as if I'm cold, but I know better. It's from fear and nothing else.

But what I don't want to admit is there are two types of alarm flowing through me.

The first is unoriginal and expected. Silvestri and his brothers have made a name for themselves in the crime syndicate. Even I'd heard of them before my rebellious episode, but I'm sure I would've anyway, since they are elite, even among the rest of the criminals in Chicago. Some say they descend—and carry pure blood—from those originating in Sicily. Other rumors insist their father was a fallen angel who was sent to prey on human women, which explains their unnatural attractiveness. I thought it was impossible.

Until the first time I laid eyes on him.

Maximus Silvestri was, and is, so beautiful he could be one of the Nephilim, or a demigod.

I thought so years ago in my youth, and I still do.

He may not have changed much physically since I first met him, except for becoming more handsome and his gaze getting more cynical but less compassionate. However, it's enough of a difference for me not to recognize him as the man I fantasized about marrying. He's grown into more power, and his body is no doubt stronger now that he's in his early thirties, but none of it matters, since the Maximus I adored is dead, killed by a lifetime of crime.

Unlike his, the changes in me have not been in my favor. Yes, my body developed into that of a woman, and I've been graced with a decent figure and average looks, but my mind...well, it has both fractured and expanded. Much to my immense shame, the episode is not a secret, and if I had any doubt as to whether Maximus knows, it was confirmed when he said I was insane.

So why does he want to marry me?

The most logical conclusion is he has a personal vendetta against my father, but I shouldn't be the asset Maximus confiscates. I've seen what most crime bosses expect to gain from their daughters: the securing of an alliance. From the way my father works his jaw from side to side and his outbursts earlier, it's apparent this is more of a hostile takeover than a truce or show of trust.

"Otello and Leone," Maximus calls out.

I jump at that, and he grips me tighter, preventing me from moving very much. Everything around me sharpens back into focus, and I silently lament the out-of-body state. I was still aware of Maximus behind me, but at least he was the only thing that held my attention, preventing me from dealing with the weighted stares of everyone else.

His chest continues to rise and fall, pressing into my spine at regular intervals, and his heartbeats do the same, pounding out a steady cadence. His cock hasn't gone flaccid, yet it's not fully erect like before. This is another part of him that pulses against me.

Two more of Maximus's men enter the room, and between them is a man who's wearing a suit and tie, carrying a brief-case. His attire is that of a lawyer about to storm through the doors of a courtroom and demand justice. In fact, he is more formally dressed than anyone else, including the groom. Maximus—who's clearly the one in charge of this situation, regardless of his choice of clothing—wears simple black slacks, Italian-leather shoes, and a crisp white dress shirt with the sleeves rolled to his elbows.

He doesn't look dressed for a simple wedding.

And neither does his bride.

My nightgown isn't sheer, but the newcomers' gazes rove over me regardless, and I stare back in a stupor. I want to rail at them, at everyone, for what's happening, but I've been conditioned to hide, to scurry back into my hole. Sometimes with a broken bone.

And always with a broken spirit.

"Good of you to join us, Your Honor," Maximus says. "Thank you for coming."

"Mr. Silvestri," the newcomer says with a nod. He places his briefcase on my father's desk and removes an opulent fountain pen along with a sheet of paper. "If you would like to look over the license before we proceed?"

Maximus releases my arm and waves his hand in dismissal. I can't help but notice he doesn't remove the one by the juncture of my thighs. "The ceremony won't take but a moment," he says. "I'm eager to take my bride home."

As if someone tossed a bucket of ice water on my father, he sputters and jabs a finger in Maximus's direction. I flinch because of the slashing movement, and Maximus's fingers tighten on my lower body. Is he warning me to stay still? I would if I could, since I have no desire for people to witness my fear.

"You have never expressed an interest in doing business with me, Silvestri, so taking Emilia doesn't make sense." My father inhales deep, and his cheeks inflate with air and more anger. "What could you possibly want with her?" He sweeps his gaze over me, and it takes everything inside me not to cringe. However, I'm not strong enough to meet my father's enraged stare, and drop my head. "Everyone knows she's ill. Are you really that much of a sick bastard you want her for no other reason than to have a plaything?"

Shame fills me, drowns me, suffocates me. Like smoke, it wraps around my body and permeates every inch of my skin and hair, entering my lungs to siphon the oxygen from them. A small wheeze escapes my lips, and my knees threaten to buckle.

"Breathe, *donnaccia*," comes the low murmur. It's so quiet I almost don't hear it. Maximus's voice releases me like a clamp loosened on a tourniquet, and blood, as well as oxygen, floods my body in a rush. I inhale through my nose while trying to maintain my composure, and the dizziness begins to recede. "Good girl," he whispers. Maximus follows this encouragement with a stroke of his thumb across my belly. Then he repeats the command, and I obey again.

But the second time, I comply for myself—not him—to hear the velvety quality of his voice as it praises me.

Receiving a gentle word from the man who obviously hates me is baffling. But not more so than the pulsing of my sex. Maximus skimmed my mons a moment ago, and I haven't been able to turn off the pleasant hum my body's emitting. Now he's caused the throbbing to intensify, and I press my thighs together to alleviate the unwanted sensation. I can't be aroused by the very person who insulted and threatened me. I blame the titillation on my innocence or even ignorance, anything as long as it's not the truth.

Or maybe I am really insane, since my sex dampened the second he threatened to fuck my mouth?

Maximus clears his throat and brings his voice back to a normal level, ending the moment of secrecy between us.

"Why, Caruso?" He clicks his tongue in admonishment, and I catch the twitching of my father's right eye. "Despite your sullied reputation, your heritage is impeccable, which means Emilia's is as well. And she is beautiful, even in her brokenness."

He makes me sound like fine china, a fragile vessel that's been hurled to the ground and shattered into pieces. Perhaps he is correct, but there is no adhesive to be found, so becoming whole will never happen. The best I can do is stab the person who steps on me.

After all, glass can be dangerous, even more so when it's nothing but shards.

Maximus brings his free hand to cup my breast, and I start to pull away but instantly freeze when he digs his fingers into my stomach and pain radiates in all directions. He fondles me through my nightgown, and my nipples harden, the ache between my legs growing. His hand on my belly relaxes, yet it's no less possessive, and where there was once discomfort, now there's heat. I want to attack him for making me respond, but instead I clench my teeth to keep from screaming in frustration. My body has betrayed me because of a couple minor touches.

And my mind would follow suit for a handful of kind words.

My father steeples his fingers, and a gleam enters his gaze. I know that look, and whatever follows will not be good. Not for me at least.

"You are correct," he says. "There are few families that have purer bloodlines than mine, so maybe we can come to some type of agreement. What do you say?"

Maximus moves his hand to my other breast while maintaining the conversation like nothing is out of the ordinary. "I'm listening."

My father wets his lips in hunger, and the action speaks of his ever-present greed. It doesn't surprise me that he's taking advantage of this hostage situation, using it for his gain. I have often likened him to a ferret due to his physical appearance and his insatiable appetite but for wealth, not food. His beady black eyes are always darting around as if searching for the best opportunity, and his nose is long and skinny and flares whenever the subject of money is brought up. It's like he can smell it. Even now, he's rubbing his hands together in anticipation.

"I've promised my daughter to another, but I am more than willing to give her to you...should you make it worth my while, Silvestri." When Maximus doesn't readily reject his proposal, my father continues. "Emilia was not born with a mental illness, so you don't have to worry about that defect passing on to your heirs. The doctor said her erratic behavior is mostly due to her mother's death, but he assured me Emilia wouldn't harm herself during a pregnancy. She's just prone to solitude and periods of sullenness, which is manageable as long as she's not put in certain social situations."

I can't recall the gasp that leaves me, nor can I stop the roiling of my stomach. My abdominal muscles cramp with severity, eliciting a stabbing pain through my center. It always happens at the thought of my mother and her demise, and I doubt that'll ever change, especially when she's mentioned by my father like just now. However, that agony is now compounded with disbelief. My father sold me to someone, and I had no idea, no inkling this was taking place. Was it Rossi? When was this going to happen?

I've never harbored illusions about my role in my father's house, since he's made that abundantly clear from the beginning, emphasizing it even more the closer I came to womanhood. But I hoped he'd given up on trying to find me a husband when I entered a year of mourning, after my actions at the gala almost two years ago. I knew it was an excuse for my unhinged behavior, but when no one offered marriage after the twelve months had passed, I thought I'd been successful in avoiding matrimony because everyone believed me to be insane. Of course, I'm the only one who knew my outburst was a ploy. Although, I suspect I'll always be haunted by the events in my past, so the assumption isn't completely inaccurate.

With my deception I wanted to buy myself some time to figure out a way to escape my father's clutches or to encourage him to disown me and remove me from his house, like Carina's father did to her. She's my only friend, and I met her at the gala two years ago. But now my window for planning and eventual freedom has closed. It has slammed in my face, and in front of an audience no less. Wherever humiliation doesn't cover me, rage is more than able to.

Like a sword that's not wielded, my anger does no damage to my enemy.

Caruso gestures to himself with a slight wave. "Clearly, I'm not mentally disabled like her. Women are the weaker sex, and she is a prime example."

"Clearly," Maximus repeats. "Who did you plan to give her to and at what cost?"

My father quickly rises to the bait, and I inwardly shake my head. Doesn't he see who's hunting him? Can't he sense the danger lurking under Maximus's calm exterior? There's no pity to be found in me as I watch my father play directly into Maximus's hands.

"To Rossi, and it was with the understanding I would obtain a spot within the Wolf Pack."

Maximus's hand stills with my nipple between his thumb and index finger. I resort to biting my lip to keep from making a sound. Whether that would be a cry or a groan, I cannot say.

"Interesting," he says in a mild tone. It contrasts with how his body tensed against mine at Caruso's words, but I'm not foolish enough to say otherwise. "Given the price, I am surprised Rossi agreed. I hadn't realized the going rate for an insane whore was so high."

Now it's me who's stiffening with indignation.

My father shakes his head emphatically, and when he rises from his chair this time, the enforcer doesn't stop him. "I don't know where you got that impression. Emilia is a virgin. I've kept her under tight surveillance, ensuring that."

Maximus doesn't answer. Instead, his hand resting on my belly snakes under my nightgown, and he dips his fingers into my lace panties. I jerk in his arms with my hair swinging wildly, trying to avoid the invasive touch, but he tightens his grip on my breast in warning, and the pain of that has me gasping. When he slides his fingers along my folds and over my clit, I bite my inner cheek until blood flows over my tongue, preventing me from groaning.

Maximus inhales sharply the moment his fingertip grazes my sex, and I know it's because of the dampness he's found there. My face flames, and I hang my head, not only in shame but so no one else in the room discovers my secret. My hair shields my face, just as my nightgown prevents everyone from seeing what Maximus is doing to my body. And my back hides his cock from view as it grows hard.

He slides his finger inside me, and I completely stop breathing. The feeling is strange, and I swear my spine is going to snap from how rigid I am. He explores me languidly, swiping my vaginal walls in a circular motion. This stretches me a little, and when my inner muscles clench in response, his cock jumps. Then he adds another finger, and I rise onto the balls of my feet, frightened by the unfamiliar pressure. Humiliation courses through my blood at the knowledge I was slick enough for the penetration not to cause discomfort.

Father Aldo mumbles the Lord's Prayer incessantly, starting in English. Then he proceeds to say it in every language he knows. I am also beseeching my maker for this to end, for him to take me from this hell.

But then Maximus strokes me in a peculiar way that has my sex quivering with desire and a moan gathering on my tongue. He quickens his pace, sending me into a tailspin as my body calls out to him, weeps for him.

Now this hell has become heaven on earth.

My orgasm builds, and I fight it with everything I have. From my mind to my heart, and down to my soul, I struggle to keep from coming undone in Maximus's arms.

"Are you fucking satisfied?" Caruso demands, the skin of his jaw tight. "If she's not a virgin anymore, it's your fault, and believe me, I'll demand recompense."

Much to my relief, Maximus withdraws his hand from my body, and I pull in lungfuls of air to keep from passing out. I brush the material of my nightgown to make sure it's back in its original position, and then I fist my hands by my sides while clenching my thighs as if that will keep him at bay.

"I believe you," Maximus says, his tone calm and emotionless.

Anger and disgust are as familiar to me as my own name. My father exhibited those emotions toward me on numerous occasions, especially after my disgraceful behavior at the gala. And Maximus did the same to me upstairs not too long ago. I know how to handle those negative feelings because they're nothing new.

But this feeling of want? This yearning for more?

I don't know how to fight my sexual attraction to Maximus, and because he's my enemy, I need to find a way. However, compared to my father, I'm hoping Maximus is the lesser of two evils.

My fallen angel dances with the devil that is Caruso.

Is it better to end up with the ruler of hell?

Or the angel who's lost his chance at redemption and perhaps his very soul?

MAXIMUS

*M*y bride's cunt was fucking wet.

I still can't get over that revelation.

"...in sickness and in health, 'til death do you part?" Father Aldo says quietly, his mumbling interrupting my thoughts. He glances at me as if I'm holding a gun to his head and waits for my response like he's not sure it'll come.

Or maybe he hopes it won't.

"I do." My voice is firm, resolute. I planned this, so there will not be any hesitation on my part.

The priest turns his focus downward to the rosary in his hands and continues on with the marriage vows, saying them as though we're at a funeral instead of a wedding. *La donnaccia* repeats the words, and I'm surprised to find her tone lacking fear, especially after everything that's occurred so far. Maybe she is insane.

That would be the only reason someone would marry me without apprehension.

"Til death do you part?" Father Aldo really asks it this time, instead of merely reciting the question from memory. Is he trying to ascertain whether this is her choice? What an idiotic notion. Emilia is no freer from this marriage than I am from my revenge. Yet someday I will obtain the justice I'm seeking.

And she will still belong to me.

She takes a deep breath. "I do."

After the vow has been said, her body relaxes in my hold. It's minute, but I'm able to detect it nonetheless. This is surprising, although it'll never be as shocking as her damp inner thighs. I didn't believe Caruso's claims about his daughter being a virgin, and why would I? He's a fucking coward that lies to save his own ass or to fuck someone else over. In this he was truthful, and it's likely never to happen again.

I've experienced the destruction he's brought about with his deceit, the underhanded deeds he's committed without remorse. And I've seen firsthand what happens when the Wolf Pack gets involved with unrest or dissension among members of the crime syndicate. In a world where thieves, murderers, and schemers thrive, there is a code, a set of laws the underworld has.

And it supersedes all others.

An entire territory full of organized crime—involving people whose intent is to circumvent the rules laid down by the government—respects the syndicate's code of honor.

There's a special type of irony in that.

It only takes one crime boss to be made an example of, and the rest fall into line like obedient soldiers waiting for their next order to be given. I've seen the methods used by the

Wolf Pack, and I respect them. Like a bull changes direction at the sight of red, a person changes their behavior at the sight of blood.

Both crimson. Both dangerous omens.

"You may now," Father Aldo says, his voice a wheeze, "kiss the bride."

Caruso crosses his arms. "About fucking time."

Ignoring everyone in the room, I turn *la donnaccia* to me. This is the first time I'm looking at her face after knowing she's a virgin, and if I hadn't felt the tightness of her cunt, I wouldn't believe it.

I grip her chin and tip it up so I can see into her eyes. "Kiss me."

She blinks up at me, and it doesn't take long for me to find the innocence lurking in their depths. She hides it well, but like opposites attract, I'm drawn to it with a force that's disturbing. Yes, her gaze was shuttered when I lifted her head, but my command weakened her defenses just enough for me to find what she desperately tries to keep hidden.

Some of her secrets remind me of my own.

This, like many things about her, is unexpected.

Emilia is careful not to touch me when she gets on her tiptoes to reach me. And my height makes this a challenge for her, since I don't bend down to assist.

This is how it will always be between us: *la donnaccia* doing my bidding.

Her lips sweep across mine, and for a second, I consider ravaging her mouth, to show her and everyone else present that she belongs to me to do whatever I will. But I've fucked around enough already by fingering her. So I grab her wrist and walk over to the desk, where the judge waits with a bored expression. Caruso beams at us as if he's truly happy to welcome me into his family, not knowing I'd skin him alive if I thought I could do it and have him survive.

"Sign here and here, Mr. Silvestri," Ben says. He hands me the pen, and without flourish I scrawl my name on the document. Then the judge turns to Emilia. "Please sign here and here, Mrs. Silvestri."

Tucking a stray curl, she presses her lips together, the ones I've discovered are softer than any others, and takes the fountain pen. Her signature is elegant, and it reminds me of my assessment of her earlier. She does act like a queen, even after I fingered her in front of her father and a man of the cloth and groped her like the *donnaccia* I named her to be.

Caruso claps his hands and grins, making his rounded cheeks all the plumper. "It's done, then. I expect we can verbalize our agreement, or would you like to have it documented?"

I hand the marriage certificate to Ben, and he locks it away in his briefcase. To the judge, I say, "You're free to go, but I expect that to be registered expediently, Your Honor." Then I turn to Caruso and cock my head. "No."

He gapes at me like a fish strewn on a beach, his jowls fluttering with his uneven breaths. I keep my features void of any emotion, but fuck me if seeing my enemy flounder doesn't bring me loads of satisfaction.

"No?" Caruso parrots.

"You are correct. There is no agreement between us. The marriage certificate is only a layer of protection if you get fucking stupid and think about going to the police." I shift my gaze to Father Aldo, who looks as if he's one step away from initiating an exorcism. "You are free to go, Father. And be sure to offer up a prayer of intercession concerning me and my bride so God will bless our union."

The priest scurries from the room, eyeing my men when he slips past them. His behavior is slightly amusing. And Caruso? He is by far the more entertaining of the two. If it weren't for Dante's weapon digging into his spine, I'm sure Caruso would attempt to shoot me with one of the guns that used to be in his desk drawer before I had my men remove them.

"What the fuck is going on, Silvestri?" He glances over to Emilia, and her entire body locks up. "Did you have something to do with this?" he asks her.

She shakes her head, and I yank her to me, causing her to careen into my torso. Her palms make contact with my chest, and she tilts her chin to look up at me in confusion. But I have my eyes set on her father. "You will not speak to her, Caruso. If you have a fucking question and wish for an answer, it'll come from me. And you," I say to Emilia without shifting my gaze to her, "will never speak to your father without my permission or you will regret it. Am I clear?"

I catch her nod from my peripheral vision, but I won't spare her a glance while my enemy is losing his shit. Caruso's nostrils flare with his every breath, and the blood has returned to his face, bringing with it a bright red as he struggles to control his anger. If only I could indulge further and torture him physically. However, I cannot steal any of that satisfaction from my brothers. It is their right as much as mine.

"You're going to fucking regret this, Silvestri!"

I finally drag my focus away from Caruso and set it on Dante. "Knock him out so we can leave, but don't accidentally kill him. His security should be rousing soon. Well, the ones who decided to cooperate."

The dull sound of metal colliding with flesh is followed by Dante's footsteps behind me as I head toward the door, my grip tight on Emilia's wrist. My men fall into line, surrounding me on all sides, and within seconds, I'm opening the door to my vehicle.

"Get in," I say to her.

She's quick to obey, and it brings back the memory of our conversation earlier about her being submissive. Emilia wasn't lying about that. As I settle beside her, I wonder how often she tells the truth.

I swing my gaze to her and slowly peruse the woman who is now my wife. If someone would've told me I'd be married to my enemy's daughter, I would've laughed and followed that by shooting them. This is un-fucking-believable, but once I heard about Rossi's official engagement to Emilia, I knew I couldn't wait any longer to put the first part of my family's revenge into motion. I didn't, and still don't, like the idea of marrying her, but knowing Caruso has now lost his coveted spot within the Wolf Pack makes it worthwhile.

Nothing in my life is going to change. I'll fuck who I want when I want, and all the while I'll continue on with the plans to destroy Caruso. The first step was to take away his daughter, who's the key to securing more power in a higher circle.

The second will be his assets.

The third will be his life.

I hoped by taking Emilia that he'd be tortured over the idea of her being abused, as well as be ridiculed by having to explain to Rossi what happened, but from Caruso's behavior tonight, I've gathered he may not care for her as much as I originally thought.

It doesn't matter though; her suffering will please me.

EMILIA

My only defense is to shut down and retreat to the deep recess of my mind, a place I always return to when I know pain is going to come. And if the gleam in Maximus's gaze is any indication, it'll be sooner rather than later.

The SUV rides smoothly, and the lights from the city fall on me briefly, turning my skin a golden color. I haven't left my room since I was eighteen years old, almost two years ago, in order to attend the gala. Or bridal auction, because that's what it truly was. So leaving behind my father's house—and more importantly my father—brings me a small amount of relief that shouldn't be present. For all I know, evil incarnate sits beside me.

Maximus Silvestri. My husband.

To say I'm still in shock over the events that just transpired is an understatement. And to say I'm scared is another one. Terrified is more accurate. Traditionally, Catholics marry for life, and this raises an important question: How long will I be allowed to live in this marriage?

"Til death do us part" never sounded so ominous.

Despite the danger I find myself in, I still can't deny the thought of never seeing my father again brings me peace. With both my parents out of my life—one by choice and the other not—I'm now an orphan. But I am free of their memories, save the ones I choose of my mother. And my father? I wish he were the one underground, not her.

Maximus may be worse than Caruso, but only time will tell. It's hard to envision someone eviler. However, based on the way my husband touched me earlier, he will want to do things to me no one has ever dared, and that is something I know nothing of.

What is considered worse is relative.

Trying not to think about such horrible things is almost impossible, and I attempt to shift my focus to the buildings passing by. How I wish I could see them in the daytime, especially the ones in the historical districts I've studied online. From the looks of it, I don't think we are anywhere near one, which is a shame. I've also browsed so many pictures of the Garden of the Phoenix I feel as if I've already been there, but I know my imagination will never replace the actual experience of walking along the trails.

Will Maximus lock me up like my father? Or is it possible that once he gets tired of me, I'll be able to visit the city and finally see some of the places I've only dreamed about?

"*Donnaccia.*"

With great reluctance and trepidation, I pull my gaze from the window only to find Maximus already staring at me. The shadows of night drift over the sculpted angles of his face, making them sharper, more pronounced. I wonder if Lucifer was this beautiful.

If so, I have a lot more sympathy for Eve's plight.

"Answer me when I call you," Maximus says. His voice is calm and soft, which worries me just as much as if he were shouting. Not that I can envision him in such an undisciplined state. If I am the epitome of submissiveness, then Maximus is that of control.

I nod, and it's minimal, as I don't want to communicate more than necessary. "How?" I whisper. His gaze narrows infinitesimally, indicating I've either shocked or irritated him with my inquiry. I drop my head in order to break free of his stare. "How am I to address you?"

From my peripheral, I take note of the way he leans further back into the leather seat, almost as if he's intrigued. He watches me with hooded eyes, and I inwardly cringe. I asked him the question in order to make sure I meet whatever expectations he has for me. It's not because I want to do his bidding, but Maximus owns me in the eyes of the underworld, and I want to make peace with him.

If I can.

He may not allow it, in which case I'll have to come up with another measure of defense against him.

"You will call me 'sir.' Nothing else," he says. "Look at me."

I lift my head. "Yes, sir."

The gleam is back in his gaze. The underlying threat Maximus constantly presents, along with my proximity to him, has my heart pounding in my ears. The space in the back seat shrinks, but I don't follow suit even though I want to curl up and disappear. The air between us is heavy with anticipation.

My breaths consist of apprehension.

His consist of excitement.

"Come here, *donnaccia*."

An invisible pressure squeezes me from all sides, and it's as if my chest caves in on itself, making each breath a struggle. I don't know this man, and I'm not sure what he considers prompt obedience, so I quickly slide closer, putting myself within his reach. Then I mentally steel myself against the likelihood of him touching me. Again.

Maximus takes a lock of my hair and rubs it between his fingers before curling the strand around his index finger. "It would seem I can no longer call you that," he says, his voice a low rumble. "You see, I was beyond certain you were a whore. Whether Rossi's or someone else's, I wasn't sure, but imagine my surprise when I found out otherwise."

He holds my gaze just as surely as he holds my hair, holds me prisoner, and holds my hand in marriage.

Or bondage.

"So tell me," he says, "what should I call you?"

I blink, not quite understanding why he asked. "What do you want to call me?"

He releases the lock of hair, and with a featherlight touch, Maximus runs his finger along the base of my throat, following the curvature of my neck. Does he feel my heart thrashing inside my ribs or notice the unsteadiness of my breaths? Once his fingertip trails the lacy edge of my nightgown, I swear he'll detect the trembling I'm trying so hard to hide.

Fear can be the only reason I speak without being prompted to do so. He pauses whenever I ask him a question, and out of self-preservation, I do it again despite risking his anger. He could interpret my inquiry as disrespect or me challenging him, but all I'm doing is trying to delay the inevitable. Maximus will touch me intimately again, and me talking won't stop him.

I've never been more certain of anything in my life.

"Fact: The abbreviation *Mrs.* originated from the word *mistress.*" I inhale deeply to remain calm, but when he dips his finger underneath the frill of lace to skim the top of my breast, I lose the oxygen I just gathered in my lungs to push it out in a stream of sentences that almost fuse together. "And the abbreviation *Mr.* was derived from *master.* Both terms evolved to carry the meanings we use now when speaking of married individuals, but they didn't start out that way. *Mistress* has many definitions, and the first is 'a woman who governs,' which is in reference to a servant. The others are 'a skilled woman,' 'a woman teacher,' and 'a beloved woman.' However, the last one is 'a whore or concubine.' So I want to know if I am a Mrs. in the married sense, or a mistress, a woman who's nothing more than used for sex?"

I pause for a moment and recall his instruction from before. "Sir," I add hastily.

My face is flaming, and some of it stems from embarrassment because I've made an idiot out of myself by spouting random tidbits of information no one cares about. But it's not only that. I'm flustered by the way his fingertip continues to glide across the expanse of my breasts, tracing the contours and coming close to my nipples. His gaze strips me naked, and there's nowhere I can run or hide that he won't find me, and I don't mean that just physically. There's something about his dark eyes and the way he studies me that make it as though he's drilling past my mental shields, discovering secrets I don't wish to tell, and finding things he doesn't have a right to know.

How can I hope to protect myself if he disarms me?

How can anyone truly defend themselves against a power greater than their own?

I have to figure out the answer. Quickly.

The weight of his stare is too much of a burden for me to maintain, and I bow my head to break the visual connection. I wish he'd do the same and take his hand away.

The silence in the space between us swells, and it's fed by the apprehension taking root in me. The only reason I don't escape to the furthest, darkest corner of my mind is because Maximus won't let me retreat. He brushes the tip of my nipple, and I flinch. It's subtle, and there's a possibility he didn't see me, but would Maximus care if he did? He repeats the same gentle caress to the other nipple, and I tug on my bottom lip with my teeth, gnawing on the soft skin to keep from reacting. I can't let him know his effect on me, but if he really wants to find out, then I won't be able to lie.

Once again my body has betrayed me.

The heat from my face travels downward and spreads, coating my arms, torso, and legs with a seductive blaze. It licks along my most sensitive parts, hardening my nipples to stiff peaks and giving a feeling of fullness to my breasts. My sex clenches, and my clit throbs, bringing my attention to the core of me that yearns for something unknown.

Well, perhaps not completely unknown.

I remember what it felt like to have Maximus stroke me and how quickly I dampened for him in spite of everything he did and said to me. The shame I experienced then has returned and is now fused with the delicious fire burning within me. I grow hotter with every inch of my skin he grazes, and I don't know how to stop it.

He retracts his hand, and the sigh of relief that rises within me is obliterated when he snakes his hand underneath my gown, the heat from his palm seeping into my thigh. There isn't a part of me that's not heightened with awareness, and it's to the point his gaze is like a physical touch as well. I can feel him watching me.

What is he searching for?

I stare at the outline of his fingers underneath my clothing, and it affirms how much larger and stronger he is than me. Maximus can take what he wants from me physically, but there has to be a way I can keep him from stealing my soul. Because the day I truly desire his touch without seduction is the day I've lost myself.

"That history lesson in abbreviations," he says slowly, "was not the answer I was looking for."

I remain still and place my focus on his words. Not his thumb stroking the inside of my thigh. Not the way my nipples ache. And not the sensitivity of my clit.

"You should know by now that you are not a wife in the traditional sense." He inches his fingers a little more up my thigh with each back-and-forth motion of his thumb. "But I don't know if I'd say you are my mistress either. That's a woman a man would seek out to avoid his wife, to fuck when he needed, and it'd be someone he didn't loathe."

"Whore. Wife," I say. "I see no difference."

Maximus's hand stills on my thigh, and the other shoots out to grip the front of my neck, using that hold to push up my head. Our gazes clash, and then he slams me into the seat so hard that my teeth click and my vision momentarily blurs. He leans over me and squeezes my throat, pressing my spine into the leather with his forearm on my sternum.

"You're right. I don't see a difference either."

The cold, flat tone of his voice is completely at odds with the glow in his eyes. The dark orbs are no longer purely black but like a bright pair of coals, burning with strong emotion. And his body betrays him, just as much as mine does. He kneads the spot above my pulse with his thumb over and over as if to soothe the restrained fury that's trying to surface in him. And the fingers from his other hand dig into the skin of my hip, yet it's almost like he's pulling me to him.

Or pulling himself closer to me.

And then he yanks my panties down with such force the material cuts into my skin, and it burns, accentuated by the ripping of silk. I'm unable to stifle the small gasp of pain, and his thumb rubs my neck deeper. I imagine it's so he can feel my reaction through the telltale racing of my heart.

I lie still and submit to Maximus because I don't want to excite him. Then I brace myself for what is to come and pray that, like a child with a new toy, he grows tired of me quickly. I also pray he doesn't break me to the point I'm no longer functional.

He slides his hand down to the juncture of my thighs, and I tense, but it doesn't keep him from wrenching my legs apart, leaving one to dangle over the edge of the seat. After shoving up my nightgown so that it's gathered in a heap on my stomach, he trains his attention on my sex that's displayed to him without restriction. The lights from outside the window reveal the flaring of his nostrils and the shuddering breath that causes his chest to shake. Fear demands I close my eyes in order to protect myself from unwanted images, but the thought of being unable to see what's coming is equally worrisome.

So I keep my eyes open and watch him touch me.

How could I have ever imagined him as my husband? What a stupid girl I was all those years ago to idolize him and fantasize about how he'd defend me against my father's wrath, and the day he'd rescue me from my lonely tower. But I am no princess, and he is no prince.

I'm a mere human, and he is an incubus, a fallen angel who is siphoning sexual energy from me to sustain himself. Maybe he's actually one of the Nephilim. Because even as I lie here, scared beyond measure, I'm still drawn to him.

He parts my folds and then grinds the pad of his thumb into my clit. I buck my hips without thought, and only his hand on my throat keeps me from dislodging his finger as he circles and presses the tiny bud. Blood fills my mouth when my teeth puncture my bottom lip, and still my whimper hits the air. The side of Maximus's mouth lifts in satisfaction.

"You may not be a whore now, but that is about to change," he says. I can barely comprehend what he's saying to me. My body convulses with electrical currents originating from pleasure. And even though I know it's from pure stimuli, I enjoy it as much as I wish it to cease.

Maybe more so.

"You will be my whore, my *donnaccia*, but it won't be for me to use your body." He brings himself close enough for his breaths to skim my flushed cheeks and to cool the perspiration on my forehead brought on by my struggles to maintain control over my arousal. "You will hate yourself for enjoying what I do to you, for knowing that you gave me something you didn't want me to have, and because you willingly played the whore for someone who would rather see you dead than alive."

He adjusts his hand so his thumb covers the entrance to my sex, and he inserts it the tiniest bit, coating the digit with the dampness he finds there. Now his smirk is fully on display, and he brings his thumb back to my clit to begin the delicious torture again. This time, I do squeeze my eyes shut.

Until his hand on my throat cuts off my air supply.

My eyelids fly open, and despite the thrashing of my body and the shaking of my legs, my gaze remains firmly fixed on his.

My tormentor.

My lover.

My husband.

With my lungs burning at the lack of oxygen, I'm no longer able to keep my hands fisted at my sides. Instead, I'm grabbing at his fingers on my throat in a weak attempt to pry them away. It's as effective as trying to remove a steel collar.

Maximus makes a soothing noise. "Relax, *donnaccia*. I didn't go through all this trouble to kill you now. Believe it or not, you will enjoy this." He waits until my nails dig into his skin and my clit is all but raw from his domineering caresses before he eases the pressure from my neck. I suck in a breath only to release it on a loud cry as my body explodes with sensation.

Pleasure assaults me, takes me prisoner, and conquers me.

I'm helpless to the tides of euphoria zipping along each and every nerve ending I possess. Maximus thrusts a finger inside my sex, and it greedily clenches around him. Shame and guilt attempt to rise but cannot overcome the orgasm wrecking me. He doesn't allow it to stop and brings about another one by massaging my vaginal walls until tears fill my eyes and glide down my temples to disappear in the loose strands of my hair splayed across the seat.

Finally he removes the hand on my neck, but I almost wish he'd left it there when he pinches my nipple. This time, it's more than one cry that pours from my mouth. His throaty chuckle penetrates the fog of sexual delirium I'm flailing in.

"Do you like the feel of your enemy's touch, *donnaccia*?" he murmurs. It's all I can do to focus enough to hear him above my panting. "Are you picturing my cock in place of my fingers?" He chooses that moment to insert a second finger into me, filling me to the point it borders on discomfort. And then he's working them in and out of my body, first with languid strokes, then with more forceful ones that have me lifting my hips.

Am I rising to meet his touch? Or am I trying to evade it?

It doesn't matter as my arousal builds to a crest, bringing with it anticipation. I want to come more than anything else in this moment and experience that all-consuming rapture once again. It is glorious, earth-shattering, and incomprehensible to someone like me, who's never felt this way.

He plays with my breasts, tweaks my nipples, and continues the punishing thrusts of his fingers. I'm on the precipice of losing myself again to his ministrations, and in this moment I don't care.

His voice is like silk and glides over me like a ribbon, a deceptive bondage that wraps itself around me. "You will only receive pleasure and satisfaction from me and no other, not even yourself. So I ask you, Do you want to come? Do you want it bad enough to beg for it?"

It's on the tip of my tongue to give him the answer he seeks. But he already has it. He knows I do and that my body is no longer my own. It's for this reason I don't give him more than he's already taken.

Even if my body cries for him, my mind screams for relief, and my soul longs for connection.

He cannot, and will not, have my supplication.

Ever.

MAXIMUS

*M*y wife comes fucking beautifully.

Damn her and fuck me.

The vehicle slows to a halt, and without looking away from Emilia, I know we've arrived at my residence. My driver exits with as much discretion as possible, and I pay him no mind. My focus is solely trained on the woman trembling beneath me.

Her cunt is so fucking wet that I'm tempted to put a third finger inside, but I hold off on that because pain is not the lesson today. Pleasure is what I want her to experience, and I want it to be to the point she is overwhelmed by it. Her body will be crazed for release, and then I plan on using it against her.

However, pain is what I'm being taught, an unintended result.

My cock is stiff and my balls are tight with the need to come. And seeing her writhe under my hands and hearing her cries aren't easing my suffering whatsoever. I knew from the moment I saw Emilia I'd be attracted to her. I like pussy; it's not rocket science. But I didn't anticipate the struggle of not fucking her.

That has to wait or it will ruin the mindfuck I've planned for my bride.

Her cunt squeezes my fingers, and I'm of half a mind to fist my cock. I mentally reinforce who she is to me—the daughter of my enemy—to keep from giving in to my primal urges. And the fact I've had to remind myself on numerous occasions over the last couple hours pisses me off. She is just one woman, and there are plenty others aside from her. Making a phone call is all it'll take to have someone running to me and spreading their thighs. But she won't do it in my bed.

I don't allow whores in it.

"You will only receive this pleasure, this satisfaction, from me and no other, not even yourself," I say, reiterating my complete and total dominion over her life. Even now, I'm in control of her orgasm, which I believe is one of her firsts. Right before she came, there was a widening of her gaze, which allowed me to see the fear that surfaced. Emilia has been anxious around me from the moment she opened her eyes to find me in her bedroom, so that is of no consequence. But this new apprehension? I traced it to the unknown. She wasn't sure what to expect, and that original expression was followed by one of awe and wonder.

Not only is my bride a virgin, but she hasn't experienced much pleasure. This information shouldn't matter one way or another. Yet it does. And that's what created this hunger in me to consume her, to ravage Emilia to the point there are no other surprises to be found when it comes to her. In our limited interactions, she has blindsided me and more than once. She creates an inconsistency, is a mystery, and that doesn't sit well.

And fuck me because I'm reluctantly intrigued.

I coat my thumb with the effect of her arousal and sweep it over her clit with severe pressure, and the hitch of her breath makes my cock jerk. "So I ask you, Do you want to come? Do you want it bad enough to beg for it?" I thrust my fingers into her again, and the liquid heat of her cunt welcomes me.

She's so close to coming. I can see it in the speed at which she exhales and feel it in the tension of her body. This may all be relatively new to her, but instinct is enough to lead her where she wants to go.

Too bad I won't let her.

I halt the movement of my fingers but leave them inside her, and she pulls her bottom lip between her teeth. The fragile skin has already been broken, and I use my free hand to run my thumb over it, releasing her lip. "Your pain, like your pleasure, will only come from me. Should you injure yourself again and deny me the right to your suffering, I will not hesitate to take it from you, many times over."

She nods, and her eyes are wild, a mixture of arousal and terror.

"Now," I say, withdrawing my hand from her face, "do you want to come?"

Her entire body shudders, making her breasts quiver and her cunt flutter. But then she doesn't move.

This will not do.

"Answer me." I punctuate each syllable with a harsh tap to her clit, which has her back bowing and her hands clenching. Emilia doesn't truly relax, but after a few seconds, she goes still. "*La donnaccia…*," I say, drawing out the words, my voice taunting.

She blinks and gnaws on her lip again. That small action has me imagining taking it between my teeth and putting my tongue on it, sucking until the wound opens again. I've thought of tasting her mouth, but kissing is an intimacy I have no interest in.

I curl my fingers, skimming the inside of her cunt. "Beg me. Tell me how much you want it, how much you need it."

Despite the fact she's clearly suffering, I don't receive a response from her. So I withdraw my hand and wipe it on her clothing. "Very well, *donnaccia*. You may think you've won, but that's far from the truth." I cock my head and hold her gaze to emphasize my conclusive thought. "Actually, I prefer it this way. Come with me."

While she sets her clothing to rights, I exit the vehicle and leave the door open for her. The instant the soles of my shoes touch the ground, I'm striding toward the house without bothering to look behind me. If Emilia thinks to run, she'll be caught by my men before she's gotten fifteen feet.

A member of my household staff greets me when I enter, and another one approaches me in the foyer. "Good evening, sir," she says in Italian.

I acknowledge her with a quick nod and switch to our native tongue. "Signora Rosetta. Is her room ready?"

"Yes, sir. And may I offer you my congratulations on your marriage?"

I grin at the woman, who is like a second mother to me. Her brown eyes are always warm and kind when she gazes at me, but that can shift in a wink. I've seen her kill someone without hesitation, and there was nothing in her gaze except satisfaction then, negating all the softness I'd thought her to possess. Rosetta has served my family since my parents were married, and it takes someone like her to survive in the underworld for so long.

"No, you may not congratulate me on my nuptials," I say, my tone playful yet exasperated, "and you know it."

Her eyes sparkle with mischief, belying her teasing, but the rest of her is composed. "I was referring to your acquisition." Her gaze darkens and roves over me when she asks, "I assume it went well?"

Rosetta's concern for me is always present. Whenever I return she assesses me for injury, and it makes no never mind to her whether I've come from murdering someone or was simply out. Her dedication falls in line with our family motto: loyalty 'til death.

And that is why she's the only woman I trust.

"Caruso's men were incompetent as expected," I tell her. "We had his place overrun quicker than I'd anticipated, show-casing his ineptitude as a boss. I was in his daughter's room before he could notify his men of our presence."

"I'm—" Rosetta snaps her head in Emilia's direction as soon as she steps inside. The older woman's shrewd gaze takes everything in, from my bride's clothes to the tousled mane of midnight curls framing her pale face, and I'm sure there's nothing that escapes her notice. "She is quite lovely, Maximus."

Rosetta brings her attention back to me, and I school my features, erasing all traces of the lightheartedness from before. I've become a master at keeping people from reading me, but sometimes Rosetta can because she knows me so well. And when it comes to Emilia, I don't want anyone knowing my inner thoughts.

"Caruso's daughter is a tool, nothing more. And as of now, she has served her main purpose." I flick my gaze over to my bride, who stands with her head slightly bowed and her hands clasped in front of that ridiculous nightgown. The pink color still irks me. Yes, she's truly an innocent, more than I thought, but she is a temptress, so that pastel doesn't suit her. "Unfortunately, I'm not certain Caruso cares for his daughter, which means any suffering she endures won't be effective. That'll disappoint my brothers."

Rosetta slowly nods. "I see. Would you like me to escort her upstairs?"

"No. She will come with me, but I'll notify you when she's to be under your supervision." I turn to Emilia, and nothing about her blank expression has changed. It looks as if she also has learned a thing or two about keeping her thoughts hidden, but that won't withstand my tactics of prying information from her.

"Very good, sir."

After dismissing Rosetta, I revert to English. "Follow me, *donnaccia*."

The quick padding of her feet across the tile confirms Emilia's obedience. It would seem she's back to being compliant, and it puzzles me. Emilia said she was submissive, yet the defiance she displayed in the vehicle was strong, more than I thought possible. What caused it to surface?

I ponder this as I lead the way to my bedroom. I'm not interested in having this interrogation in my office, though I'm not exactly thrilled about her being in my personal domain. But I want to use the intimate setting to fuck with her mind, to make her think about what I could do to her. In reality, I could do anything at any location and at any time. And if I did, at what point would she finally beg?

When I asked her if she wanted to come, it was all I could do to keep from fucking her into giving me a response. We both knew how desperate she was, but my bride wouldn't give in, and that was with the knowledge I could've punished her for it. Because she's avoided rebellion this entire time, I'm puzzled over what prompted her change in behavior.

Even more so over the fact I was aroused by it.

I may have to fuck her out of my system, but the filth she comes from still flows in her blood, and I don't know if I can reconcile that, even to clear my head. She is tainted, no matter her innocence.

After I push open the door, I gesture to the bed with a flick of my wrist. "Sit."

Emilia enters, and I study her reaction to the space. She roams her gaze over the raised platform, which displays my large bed, complete with crimson bedding that's dark enough to be mistaken for black. The high ceilings give the room a colossal feel, as do the floor-length bulletproof windows decorated with sheer curtains.

Once she's seated on the edge of the mattress with her hands folded demurely in her lap, I remove my weapons from their holsters and set them on the nightstand—a test to see how foolish she is. They aren't within reach yet not more than five feet away. Emilia doesn't do more than watch me with a wary expression, and not once does her body lean toward the firearms.

"Tell me everything you know about Caruso's operations," I say. I unbutton my shirt and remove my holsters with her gaze fastened to my every move. "It doesn't matter how insignificant the details; I want them all."

"I don't know anything."

I click my tongue at her in admonishment. "You know more than you think, and I have no problem forcing the information out of you. And don't forget to address me appropriately."

She licks her lips, most likely due to nervousness, and it snags my attention. "I wasn't told anything concerning his business dealings, and I wasn't allowed to leave my room, so there's no way I would've been able to find out, sir."

"Fucking useless." I toss my shirt to the floor and remove my shoes. Then I reach for my belt and undo the clasp, threading the leather through the buckle. "I didn't think you were the type to lie and be difficult, but I'm not above breaking you of that stubborn streak."

Her eyes widen and then bounce around the room as though looking for a way to escape. She glances at the weapons lying on the nightstand, but there's more apprehension in her gaze than interest. Although, I'm sure she'd be happy to shoot me if given the chance.

I wouldn't have it any other way.

The idea of punishing her excites me, but the fact my cock hardens and has me wanting to fuck her for pleasure is not acceptable. If it doesn't bring about her suffering, then I won't do it…

"I'm not being stubborn, sir," she says, her gaze vacillating between me and the belt in my hands. "I really don't know. Ask me anything else and I'll tell you. I swear it."

I go still, and so does the rise and fall of her chest. Emilia stops breathing whenever she waits for me to respond. It's one of her tells, along with her lip biting. She may think she's keeping everything hidden from me, but that's far from the truth.

"Where would your father keep vital information hidden?" I ask.

She inhales, drawing my gaze to her breasts. I grip the belt until the leather bends in my palms and my knuckles turn white. I'm so focused on repressing the urge to touch her that I stare at her, taking in every detail of her face with great scrutiny. It was not something I paid attention to, since I already had pictures confirming her identity.

Those photos are nothing compared to seeing her in person.

A tiny crease forms on her brow, and she drops her gaze, making it so her lowered eyelids and long lashes keep her eyes hidden from me. The color in her cheeks is slowly returning, and her lips are still swollen, giving them a hue that's rosier than usual. There wasn't enough light in her bedroom or in the SUV to see her as clearly as I do right now, and I didn't pay attention to her in Caruso's office or in my foyer. I'm drinking her in like I've never seen her before.

And like a drink, she's intoxicating.

"I believe he has a safe in his bedroom," she says. "If there is anything of interest to be found, it'll be there." Emilia raises her head to meet my gaze, giving me an unobstructed view of hers. "My mother used to warn me to never go in there even if it was empty."

"What else?"

My words come out rough and deep, and I clear my throat to relieve it from the gruffness brought on by arousal. Her eyes are green. It's a brilliant shade of emerald that's shining due to the anxiety she's feeling at my interrogating her. The hue is contrasted greatly with the ebony hair framing her face, which makes her eyes stand out all the more. I can't believe I didn't notice prior to this.

She taps her thigh in obvious agitation. "Fact: Most people hide their valuables in places they habitually congregate, which implies he could have other vaults located in his office or the billiard room."

I shake my head to clear it, and her arched brows rise a fraction, showcasing her worry. Apparently she believes my action implies I don't find her answer satisfactory, and it's better for her to assume that than know I was temporarily distracted by her beauty.

"Perhaps. Why didn't Rossi marry you sooner?" I ask.

Her mouth thins. "What?" At my glower, she averts her gaze. Again. "I mean to say that...my father and he agreed it was best I honor the traditional year of mourning after my mother's passing. I'm not sure why Rossi waited for another year after that."

I've been curious about the circumstances surrounding Emilia's engagement to Rossi but never more so than right now. Asking her is pointless, as she won't reveal anything because she doesn't seem to know anything. However, it's imperative I find out. The most likely reason for the marriage is so Rossi and Caruso could become allies, which Emilia's father already confirmed.

And because she is beautiful.

Did that have anything to do with Rossi's decision? Caruso may be my enemy, but Rossi is also under the watchful eye of my family, and if he wants Emilia, I could use her as leverage.

"Did Rossi ever talk about fucking you?" I ask.

At hearing the words out loud, they heat my blood almost to its boiling point, which is laughable because I'm the one who wanted to know. But the very idea of Rossi taking her cunt...

That is not an option.

EMILIA

I shake my head so forcefully it causes a few tendrils to slap my cheeks. "No, Rossi didn't say such things. The only time I spoke to him was at a gala two years ago, and it was only once. My father secured our engagement, but I wasn't aware of that until tonight, sir."

What I don't say is that Rossi disgusted me and I'm glad to be rid of him. However, trading him for another monster is not what I had in mind.

Silence is my only ally unless Maximus demands I speak, and considering the topic, I'm not sure I'll be able to. Inside my mind there's a chant, a mantra that starts as a whisper and grows in volume. It's always been there, and usually it's so low I can't hear it past the internal screams, but now it's begging me to listen.

Submit to survive. Envision an escape. Leave and never look back.

How I wish I were a sparrow so I could fly away or a wolf so I could fight my way to freedom. Instead, I'm nothing more than a timid creature whose inclination is to scurry away and hide. And my husband is undoubtedly a predator, one that could snuff out my life with a single attack.

Maximus's mouth pulls to the side in contemplation. "I'm sure Rossi did talk about his physical interest in you but obviously not with you present."

There's nothing for me to say to that, unless I were to voice my agreement. My father has never respected women, and I've heard him say awful things to and about them. I assume the only reason I never heard anything concerning Rossi was because I was locked away in my room. Although I suffered in some ways by being denied a normal amount of human interaction, being in solitary confinement was the greatest blessing under the circumstances.

I wish Maximus would ignore me like my father did most of my life.

Instead, this man towering over me has paid too much attention to me. And my body. Heat burns just underneath the skin of my cheeks whenever I think about what happened in the car with him. I may not have a choice in what he does to me, or my physical response to it, but my thoughts on the subject? Those shouldn't be anything except full of revulsion.

Yet that was not the case.

Even now, it's a struggle to keep my thoughts in line and on the matter at hand, which is why I've concentrated on his mouth, waiting for him to speak again. A little bit ago, my gaze drifted from the leather belt in his fingers—the same ones he used to fuck me with—to his erection, and I didn't hear the question he asked. I can't afford to make that mistake again. However, after feeling the length of him pressed against me, I couldn't squelch my curiosity and amazement.

The research I did on the internet during my captivity was an incredible amount. I wanted to learn everything about anything, including sex. Certain websites were prohibited to me, but anything educational was permitted. The medical texts concerning sexual organs, arousal, orgasms, and reproduction assisted me a lot and were most assuredly not part of my online curriculum.

But that information did not, in any way, shape, or form, prepare me for what Maximus made me feel.

He takes a step toward me, and I shift my gaze from the beautiful tattoo on his hand to his bare chest. This is another distraction able to scatter my thoughts. The muscles along his torso are finely honed with each divot sharp and defined. Whenever he moves the slightest bit, they flex or ripple, and I have to look away or be caught staring. Maximus doesn't need to know about my attraction to him, and I'm hoping it'll soon wither and die.

I start at the sensation of an object landing against the underside of my jaw and jerk my gaze upward to find his already on me. My throat nudges the edge of the belt when I swallow deep and valiantly struggle to hold on to my composure.

"Did you hear what I said?" he asks.

I mentally scramble to provide an answer but come up empty. Once again he's caught my mind wandering away with my thoughts, and I can only hope he doesn't know the reason. If he did, Maximus would use my attraction to torture me more than he already has. Yet I suspect he hasn't truly begun the worst of it.

I shake my head. "No, sir."

"If I have to repeat myself again, you'll find this belt across your ass, not resting under your chin. Am I clear, *donnaccia?*" At my nod, he narrows his gaze at me. "Was the orgasm I gave you on the way here one of your firsts or not?"

That was the question?

I bunch the material of my nightgown in my fists and then squeeze to keep from trembling. Humiliation and indignation war within me, but I can't let either of them win. Maximus expects an answer, and I have to give him one. But which? The lie that says I've touched myself on several occasions? I'm not sure he'd believe me, and telling him it was done by another man may not be the best response either. Maximus doesn't care about me, but I'm his property, and I have to consider the idea he'd be upset if someone played with his toy before he did.

However, the truth is almost too embarrassing to admit. How can I tell him I've never done that to myself because I didn't want to put on a show for my father's men? How can I explain I used to fantasize about him, my fallen angel, doing that and much more to me?

I drop my gaze to avoid his. Just that submissive action fills my stomach with nausea, but it won't compare to the words on my lips. "It was my first orgasm."

What will Maximus do to me now that he knows?

The belt falls away from underneath my chin, but there is no relief. Especially not when I detect the arrogance in his voice. He is prideful, much like Lucifer was.

And like the devil, I hope Maximus's downfall is eternal.

"I thought as much," he says. "Take off your gown."

My eyes close of their own volition at the command. So it begins.

After uncurling my fingers, which now ache from me clenching them tightly, I slide off the mattress. My feet land on the plush carpet, and I pull the sleepwear up and over my head. Remaining in only my bra and panties is the same as being nude for me. I haven't been undressed in front of anyone in years, and even the henchmen at my father's house weren't allowed to see into the bathroom connecting to my bedroom. It was the only place I truly had any privacy, but if I stayed in there too long, then someone would come looking for me, so I never lingered more than necessary.

I tuck my chin to avoid Maximus's gaze, since I have no desire to see his look of satisfaction due to my shame. My hair creates a flimsy curtain around my face as I struggle to keep silent. The urge to plead for mercy burns in my throat, and I wrap my arms around my middle as if that will help. It doesn't.

The crack of the belt against my forearm has me sucking in a breath originating from surprise more than pain. I jerk my head up before I can stop myself and rub the stinging away from the spot that was struck.

"Don't hide your body from me," he says. "It belongs to me, not you. Put your hands down by your sides and keep them there until I say otherwise."

I lower my arms in an automatic fashion while snared by the look in his gaze. The black of his eyes gleams the same way it did in the car, and I suspect something more than excitement shines there. Lust is there too, and I find it odd he's aroused by me. Is it normal to be attracted to someone you hate? If his behavior, along with his stiff cock, is any indication, it's happening whether normal or not.

At least it's not just me.

He narrows his gaze a second before the strand of leather slaps my thigh. The skin throbs, and I squeeze my elbows to my sides so I don't massage the area.

"What did I say about acknowledging me when I speak to you, *donnaccia?*"

"My apologies, sir."

His dark hair falls across his brow when he tilts his head. "Your skin turns pink quite easily. Do you bruise quickly as well?"

"No, sir."

"We'll see." He circles me with the belt in hand, finally breaking our connection so I can drop my gaze. Starting just below my backside and dragging it down, he runs the leather strap along the seam of my thighs. "Spread your legs."

I obey and nearly jump when he gathers my hair and tosses it over my shoulder to undo the clasps of my bra. Then he brings his arm around me to trace a finger along the lacy fringe covering my breasts. The bra isn't heavily padded and offers no protection from his thumb as he glides it across my nipple. The heat of his body pours onto mine, and his breaths skim the shell of my ear, making me stiffen. His erection sits in the groove of my ass, and when he plucks the bra away from my chest, his cock grinds into me.

"Remove it completely," he says.

Am I imagining the way his voice has become thick or the way his breaths are slightly uneven? His composure is slipping, and I'm not sure if that's a good thing.

The only problem is my composure is slipping also.

I know I don't have much to fortify me, but I gather the remaining fragments of my resolve and use them to create a mental wall. It holds steady while he fondles me and runs his fingers along my cleavage. Despite the goose bumps breaking out all over me, I believe I can maintain this barrier and protect myself from him.

Until he grabs me between the legs, cupping my sex, and hauls me back to slam against his torso. Skin to skin is intimate, and I'm simultaneously puzzled and frightened by it.

I hate that I crave his touch as much as I condemn it.

"What am I to do with this cunt of yours, hmm?" he murmurs in my ear, his voice a seduction all on its own.

Does he expect an answer? My mind is firing off warnings, making it hard for me to summon a coherent thought, but I don't want to feel the pain of his belt, so I blurt out the first thing I think of.

"You're going to do whatever you want, so I assume you don't care to hear the truth from me. In fact, if I were to give you a suggestion, it could result in the opposite outcome I hope for. Have sex with me or leave me be, but whatever you choose, it won't be because I encouraged you. This choice, as well as its consequences, is yours." I inhale sharply at having forgotten to address him and quickly add, "Sir."

The muscles of his torso twitch as though he's suppressing laughter. Or anger. I squeeze my eyes shut, since he's behind me and can't see. Then I prepare for his reaction, unsure of what's to come.

"*Donnaccia*, that is not what I expected. But I'm finding that to be true about you, more often than not."

He runs his thumb over my clit, outside my panties, and I pull my bottom lip between my teeth and bite down to stifle the sounds that almost tumble from my mouth—the ones that would give him the satisfaction he's wanting. My lip is already sore from what I did to it earlier, but considering the way Maximus touches me, it won't be long until I give in to whatever response he's searching for.

I'm not sure whether to be relieved or surprised when he withdraws his hand. Perhaps both. This entire situation is not something I can wrap my mind around. Maximus scares me just as much as he excites me, and I may not be insane in the sense I can't function, but I think I am crazy for vacillating between wanting him to touch me and being repelled by it.

I developed an aversion to human contact, yet my husband has forced it on me to the point I've learned to cope. And it was a complete submersion because Maximus has touched me nonstop since I first saw him in my room.

The soft leather now hovering just above me snags my gaze, and I follow it as Maximus lowers and secures the belt around my neck. "This will keep you in place when you struggle," he says. With a sharp tug on the strap, it tightens, encircling my throat like a collar. Then he brings my back flush to his chest and slides his free hand into my panties.

"You're fucking wet," he rasps, circling my entrance. He thrusts a finger inside me, then curves it, massaging the walls of my sex. The leather bites into my neck when I jolt forward, and he clicks his tongue at me. "I knew you'd try to run, but you'll never get free."

His words settle over me, and combined with the gruffness of his tone, they make me writhe in his hold. My muscles clench around his finger, and pleasure shoots through me, increasing with him touching my clit. The moan I've kept hidden this whole time slips past my lips, and Maximus pulls on the belt until the back of my head rests on his shoulder. He places his mouth just beside my ear, and I stare up at the ceiling, unseeing, lost in sensation.

"I won't let you go until you ask me to come, *donnaccia*. However long it takes, whatever pain is necessary, you will suffer, and then you will be on your knees, using those lips to fucking beg me."

A whimper that is partially fear and arousal escapes me. Everything is too much. In the car, Maximus touched me, but it wasn't with the entire length of his body pressed to mine. It wasn't with his cock rubbing against me, dredging up fantasies to entice me into imagining what it'd be like to have him inside me. This experience is more heightened than the previous, and I'm worried I'll lose myself in his embrace to the point I do beg him.

I can't keep my body from him, but my will is mine.

It's just never waged war with someone whose very presence ignites me.

He flicks his tongue in my ear right before his warm, unsteady breaths skim it. "How many fingers can you take in this tight cunt of yours? Two?" He inserts another finger inside me, and my hips lurch from the feeling of fullness. "What about three?" This time there is discomfort, but it's quickly replaced with something I can't describe. My sex fists him, and tremors wrack my body, snaking along its entirety as my ecstasy grows.

"Ask me," he growls, his nose and mouth brushing my temple. "I know you're fucking close."

I dig my nails into my thighs, and it's enough to keep me from turning my head to give voice to my plea. He didn't win when he touched me before, and he won't now. But the strain has my breaths uneven and thin, along with my heart thrumming so loudly in my chest I fear it will explode. Logic says it won't, but logic is nowhere to be found. Only pleasure is here, and it demands to be had. And fed.

He withdraws his fingers from me, and I sag in his embrace, uncaring of the belt digging into my throat with my every swallow. I close my eyes, unable to do anything else, and wait for the next round of exquisite torture. He said he wouldn't give up, so I know not to expect something different.

"On your knees," he says.

I slowly sink to the floor, thankful the belt has enough slack to allow me to do so without choking. Keeping my head bowed is both smart and dangerous. It could be best to let him think I'm submitting to him, which I am but only physically. Or it could be dangerous if he sees that as me avoiding him. Which I'm also doing.

His steps are barely discernible when he circles me in a stalking manner. The belt around my neck rotates, making it very clear what his position is to me. As if I can't feel him nearby, lighting up my receptors. Then his bare feet enter my line of vision—which is focused on the tiny fibers of carpet— and stop directly in front of me. He yanks on the leather, causing my chin to lift, and I bring it up higher until I'm staring at him.

In this position, I truly feel like he is my master and I'm his mistress.

Mr. and Mrs., in every sense of the words.

"You told me you submit, *donnaccia*. Yet you refuse to ask that I let you come. I want to know why?"

Maximus is painfully beautiful to look at, especially when he gazes at me, his dark eyes silently demanding my secrets. "I don't want it, sir." The truth hangs in the air, denser than fog and heavier than metal. "It's…" I shake my head and inhale deep. "I wasn't prepared for this."

He drops the belt, and the loose end falls to lie between my breasts. Uncertainty is like a second skin to me and has been ever since I opened my eyes to find him idling in my room. Only, it's worse. If I could just make him tire of me, or want to be rid of me like my father, I'd be free enough to plan my escape. I knew I was somewhat safe from Caruso, since he didn't readily kill me after the gala, but there is no such guarantee with Maximus.

"What can I do…" My words die on my tongue at the sight of him undoing his pants.

He squints down at me. "What can you do? I think you already know the answer to that."

Panic kick-starts my heart into full throttle, and it crawls in my throat when he steps out from the last of his clothing. His cock fills my gaze, and I quickly avert it. The medical texts made sex sound simplistic and natural, but that is not the impression I'm getting right now.

I briefly close my eyes as if it'll remove the image right in front of me, the one now seared in my brain. "If I beg, will you leave me alone?" I whisper.

From my peripheral, I watch Maximus bring his hand to me, and I brace for impact. He surprises me by taking my chin between his thumb and index finger. His grip is tight, and his gaze is sharp, shredding the last bit of courage I have left.

"Have you ever played chess, *donnaccia*? If you had, you would know you've just given me your queen, your greatest asset, leaving you nothing stronger to fight me with." He smirks at me, and my stomach churns. "It is only a matter of time before you concede, and I say checkmate."

"My queen, sir?"

He nods. "Yes, you have given me insight as to what you want, which is to be left alone. And that is the one thing I will never offer you, now that I know."

Defeat streaks through me like the tip of a knife, slicing deep into my soul and leaving it to bleed. How could I have been so stupid to give myself away like that? My body offers a response I don't want to acknowledge. I'm yearning for his touch just as much as I want him to leave me be.

But until he dismisses me, I will remain here, in the chasm of my own desire where nothing makes sense and everything feels divine.

Maximus lowers his hand from my face and brings it to his cock, curling his long, elegant fingers around the length. He grips it, and the head glistens with a tiny bead of arousal. "You will always be bested by me. It'd be wise for you to realize that here and now, and perhaps I will prolong your life. For a time." He steps forward, positioning his cock less than a breath away from my mouth, and takes the belt in his unoccupied hand. "Take my cock between your lips, but know you'll wish you were dead if you decide to injure me."

I open my mouth, and he's quick to thrust into it. His groan is nothing like I've ever heard, and even when he speaks, his voice is little more than a growl. "Make me come and maybe I'll leave you in peace tonight."

My sex dampens, my arousal returning with a vengeance. I close my lips fully around him and suck hesitantly at first, but when he closes his eyes and hangs his head, I become more aggressive. The salty taste of him spreads across my tongue as I swirl it around the tip, alternating that with hard pulls of my mouth. Maximus weaves his hand in my hair and cups the back of my neck to guide my movements. The belt is all but forgotten except for the way his knuckles go pale from the force of his grip on the leather.

I take everything in, starting with the scent of his skin and ending with the taste of him. But I mostly watch his face. It contorts with a pained expression, and his thrusts increase in speed. His groans have my fingers twitching with the need to touch my clit, to ease the ache that's unbearable at this point. He's brought me so close to orgasm on several occasions after the first one, and now that I know what's possible, I want it so badly that I devour his cock for the chance to be alone and see to my needs.

It's not the only reason. I want to drive him insane with desire. I want to see if I can elicit the same response in him that he brought about from me. And mostly, I want to see that moment, that second of vulnerability cross his face and flood his gaze when he comes.

Because of *me*.

A stream of air shooting between his teeth forms a hiss, and then another groan rumbles from his chest that's dotted with perspiration. The tiny droplets outline the muscles that are hardened from sexual tension, and his biceps are strained from his grip on me and the belt. He lets go of the strap and threads his fingers in my hair, one hand right beside the other to clasp my head and then to cradle it.

Why is he holding me in such a way? It could be to ensure he can readily dislodge me from him should I choose to hurt him, but it doesn't feel that way. His touch is...light. Definitely full of anticipation fused with agony but not anger or punishment. Does he expect that gentleness from me? And do I want to touch him?

My hand trembles as I reach out and tenderly skim the underside of him.

"Fuck yes," he rasps.

I cup his sac and massage it in my palm while trying to keep my throat relaxed as he plunges his cock deeper than before. I continue my exploration of him, and he spreads his legs, making it so I can reach him fully. Hesitation worms its way past my desire dripping down my thighs, past his enticing groans, and past my sore jaw. I don't know what he wants or what's allowed, so I graze his perineum with my nails and then gently rub the area. His hips thrust forward, and I snatch my hand away.

He blows out a harsh breath. "More."

Does he realize he asked me for something? And it's close enough to be considered begging?

It looks as if the king, while being the most important piece on the chessboard, is still the most vulnerable.

Even to a pawn like me.

MAXIMUS

I fuck Emilia's mouth, wishing it was her cunt.

This enrages me, but I'm too close to coming to give a shit. All I know is this pretty mouth of hers feels better than I thought it would given her inexperience. Maybe it's her hesitancy that turns me on, or it could be the soft touch of her fingers gliding over my skin. Whatever the reason, I grit my teeth and open my eyes to keep my orgasm from arriving before I've had a chance to see my cock buried between her rosy lips. They are bright with color from the friction of my cock going in and out, and fuck if that doesn't make my balls tight. There's a tiny furrow to her brow as if she's concentrating on the task, and her enthusiasm confuses me. I can't think about it, nor can I dwell on how she voluntarily touched me for the first time.

It shouldn't fucking matter.

But it *does*.

I shove all thought aside, exchanging it for the feel of her taking me deeper than before. Her eyes widen when the head of my cock taps the back of her throat, and something about that expression does me in. My cock swells, and my orgasm rages through me. My thrusts are almost feral as I plunge into her mouth, forcing her to swallow. She does without a grimace or a trace of disgust.

That fucks me up.

Haven't I done enough horrendous things to this woman already? They aren't as bad as I originally planned, but they are not kind either. She should hate me, completely and totally, like I do her, like I want her to reciprocate. Yet Emilia doesn't carry the darkness in her gaze I expected to see. The green of her eyes is filled with apprehension, fatigue, and… lust. That is what makes them shine as brightly as a candle's flame.

Why does she always do the unexpected?

That is what makes her a problem.

But tonight she is my solution.

I slowly and reluctantly pull my cock from her mouth, and she licks her swollen lips. I bite back a growl. If I didn't know she's a virgin, I'd seriously think she was fucking with me right now. Emilia is sex personified with her soft skin, shapely curves, and delicate features, but her cunt is unblemished.

It begs to be fucked.

By me.

So why do I hold off? Because I want her to yield to me, to beg me, her owner. She called me her master in the car by informing me of the origin of the abbreviation *Mr.*, and I wanted to take her then. Now she's taken me inside her mouth, a part of her body, and it's not enough. If I am the master, then why do I want to give in to her, my slave?

I probe Emilia's gaze with mine, and she turns away, her midnight hair catching the dim lighting of the room, which makes it shine. She can't ever return my stare without retreating in some way, and I'll allow it for now. However, she didn't close her eyes or look away when I came in her mouth. My cock stiffens at the mental picture.

"Get up," I say.

She lifts her head, and her lips part at my erection. I'd shove it in her mouth again if she hadn't acted amenable to the idea earlier. Would she be just as accepting if it was between her legs instead of her lips? Tonight is not the time to find out. I planned to get her to submit, and Emilia won't sleep or eat until she does.

She winces as she rises into a standing position. Her knees are red from the floor, and the hue matches her lips. That color on her ass will fit in nicely with the duo. I remove the belt from around her neck and fold the length of it in half while I gauge her reaction. She watches the strip of leather like it's a serpent ready to strike, and it's as if she's read my mind.

I jut my chin toward her lace panties. "Remove those and give them to me."

She does, and I swallow when she bends down. The action gives me a glimpse of her cunt and drags my gaze to the swaying of her rounded breasts. Her nipples are pebbled, and she shifts her weight after handing me the piece of lace.

"Still not ready to beg?" I ask. I run my thumb over the section that was molded to her crotch, and the scent of her hits my nose, making my nostrils flare. It is intoxicating. My smirk from earlier returns, mostly from amusement but also from satisfaction. "This material is soaked, *donnaccia*. Tell me why."

She opens her mouth and then closes it. That is due to either indecision or stubbornness, but I won't allow the latter. I bend my arm and then swing it in her direction so the belt slaps against her ass cheek and part of her thigh. Emilia twitches and lets out a gasp.

I relish her reaction as well as the blushing of her skin. "Tell me why this lace is fucking drenched. Now."

She licks her lips, and that distracts me as well as makes my cock jump. This torture is far from one-sided, but at least I can say she will suffer more than I.

"You've manipulated my body by touching it in ways that stimulate it to the point of arousal," she says. "From there, it's only a matter of continuously doing the same thing until the body reaches its peak of sexual pleasure. You're using a basic part of biology to gain a reaction from me physically. So the answer is my sex is lubricating itself in preparation for penetration, a way to ensure the coitus between myself and another can be without too much, or no, discomfort. Arousal is also a way to encourage intercourse between a male and female, since her libido may not be as high. I believe this to be true of us."

She points to my cock. "Take your erection, for example. It happened so quickly and without much stimulation after you ejaculated. Speaking of, a woman's orgasm is thought to assist in conception by moving the sperm through the uterus. As I said, this is the science behind biology being used as a way to punish me for whatever my father did, because you want to or for some other reason I'm not aware of and probably never will be." She takes a deep breath. "Sir."

Un-fucking-believable.

This young woman is either truly insane or so intelligent that she's oblivious to social norms. I can't push past my bafflement at her answer. From the beginning, I wanted her to be terrified of me so I could absorb that emotion, revel in the idea of Caruso's daughter, his only child, being tormented. I run my gaze over her, and I'm unable to detect anything from her beyond apprehension.

And lust. That is still there.

She shifts her weight from one foot to the other, and it's done so covertly I'd miss it if I weren't paying attention. I know this tiny movement is due to her cunt wanting the very things Emilia just dispassionately described. Biology may be at work, but those terms—*intercourse* and *orgasms*—are not correct.

La donnaccia wants to be fucked, and she wants to come.

I toss the undergarment aside, and she watches the object plummet to the floor. What is she thinking about? And after that last response, do I really want to know? Fuck. I do. Her mind, warped or not, intrigues me. She never does or says what I predict, and this mystery goads me to learn more and figure her out. If this is not her true personality, then she won't be able to keep up the facade forever.

Nor will she be able to keep from begging.

"Get on the bed," I say, gesturing to it with a flick of the belt. "I want you to stay on your knees but have your chest flush to the mattress."

My fingers twitch with the urge to prod her so she'll move quicker. Everything Emilia does is with forethought, and that comes across in her deliberate mannerisms as well as her words. Holy shit is it in her words.

Emilia approaches the bed with a hesitancy that is easily seen in the rigidity of her spine and the tenseness of her extremities when she places her knee on the mattress. I drink in the sight of her ass in the air, pink from the bite of leather, but at the glimpse of her cunt on display in such an inviting position, I fist my cock and bite back a groan.

She will surrender to me and despise herself for it, or my revenge won't be complete.

The instant the leather makes contact with the back of her thigh, Emilia sucks in a breath. That tiny reaction tells me how nervous she is, and I enjoy it. I drag the belt to slide along her ass and up the small of her back, saying, "I give you permission to speak whatever is on your mind, and I promise not to punish you for it unless you become uncontrolled. So tell me, what are you thinking?"

I find myself full of anticipation and circle the bed to stand where I can easily see her face. Her gaze is fixed on the comforter as if it fascinates her, but I doubt that's the reason. I replace the feel of the belt with my hand to brush the long, inky strands of her hair off her spine and to the side. They blend in with the red color of the bedding, since it's nearly black, and her skin is a beautiful contrast. It's a cream surrounded by dark hues that make it appear porcelain. I know for a fact it's just as delicate.

"*Donnaccia?*"

Her mouth thins. "I'm not thinking about anything in particular, sir."

81

"Lies do not become you. If another one flows past your lips, you will regret it."

Her words come out in a rush, and if I weren't facing her, I wouldn't hear all of them.

"I'm thinking about the belt and how much it's going to hurt," she whispers. "I'm thinking about how my humiliation is just beginning, which means I need to grow accustomed to it now. I'm thinking how unfair my life has been and wondering if God only answers the prayers of men. I'm thinking about the best way to get you to...finish whatever this is. And I'm thinking if it really matters, since tomorrow will bring more of the same."

She exhales, and it's different from the ones earlier. It is full of something deeper and darker than defeat. It's...acceptance. I know there's fight in Emilia, because she showed it to me by refusing to grovel, so what's happening exactly? Are her words merely a ploy to gain my sympathies? Emilia is certainly clever enough, but I'm not sure that's what this is.

I flick my wrist, and the belt cracks against her ass cheek. She cries out, but it's muffled by the bed, and afterward she presses her lips together and squeezes her eyes closed. To shut out me and the rest of the world.

That's not fucking happening.

"Open your eyes," I snap. She obeys, giving me an unobstructed view of the emotions in her gaze. It's been decades since I've been anything but blind with rage, yet I easily recognize the vulnerability in her. It snags my attention longer than I'd like before I'm able to dismiss it. "That slap wasn't executed with all my strength," I say, "so you'd do well to consider yourself fortunate. Although, you deserve a more

82

severe reprimand, seeing as you've forgotten to address me appropriately on several occasions."

"I apologize, sir."

Her voice is dull, lifeless. At hearing it, a twinge that goes beyond annoyance coils within my gut, and I'm not able to readily identify it. Or why her sounding that way disconcerts me.

"Are you ready to ask me for what you're needing?" I tilt my head. "Maybe if you ask me to bring it to God, he'll give you an answer."

Emilia's gaze flickers to mine, and a spark of defiant anger has her green eyes glimmering. It makes my cock harder than the blushing of her ass or the way her cunt is spread. She's been hiding this inner strength by looking away or keeping her eyes downcast, but not any longer. I wish to fully see this rebellious spirit at all times, because this is the challenge I've been waiting for.

I quirk a brow. "Your silence is damning."

With intense focus, I whip the belt across her ass, bringing the flush to her other cheek. I repeat the motion twice more in different locations, spreading the blushing hue across her entire backside. She bites her lip but manages to keep her gaze on me the entire time, even when she winces. I lean onto the bed and palm one ass cheek, letting the heat from it seep into my palm.

"I don't care which one comes first, but know this: you're either going to beg me to stop or to come. Those are your only options." I slide my fingers along her skin until they graze the lips of her cunt. As one would handle a stringed instrument, I thrum my fingers over her folds. "You should be grateful to have a choice."

My bride's petite frame trembles, the shaking magnifying the moment I skim her clit. "You lied, you know," I say, dipping my finger inside her cunt to coat it with the moisture I find there. Then I circle her tiny bud with agonizingly slow strokes until her hips lean into my palm. A tiny surrender but not enough.

If it's not complete, then it's not satisfying.

"You said you submit to people," I say, my gaze locked onto hers, not wanting to miss any of her reactions. "You're willing to give me your body; that much is clear. But your mind?" I shake my head and lightly pinch her clit at the same time. She gives a lusty moan, and I know that cost her a bit of pride. "Your mind is hidden from me, and the barrier around it is formidable. Is insanity what keeps you protected? Or intelligence? Perhaps it's something as simple as solitude?"

I flick and rub her clit until she's barely able to keep her eyes open, and even so, they are clouded with fierce desire. She digs her fingers into the bedding and her thighs go taut every couple strokes, as if she's coaxing her orgasm to emerge. I don't think she can stop herself.

Her cry hits the air when I slip my fingers inside her, and with me hovering over Emilia's back, I'm able to experience every convulsion that travels through her. Another muffled groan, one full of frustration that rivals despair, spills from her, and I know she's just about to break.

"Beg me," I whisper. I bring my mouth to her ass cheek and nip at it, directly over the still-pink flesh, and she grinds into my hold. "Tell me you want this."

"I—" The choked sound is cut off by a spasm. I still my fingers, taking note of the clenching of her cunt and the pulsing of her clit. Emilia's about to burst, yet she won't yield.

I switch tactics and retract my hands to grip her hips and flip her onto her back. She stares up at me with a dazed expression, and her legs fall listlessly to the sides, an unintended offering of her sex. She blinks rapidly when I slide my hands underneath her body to grip her ass and then lower my head to nibble on her clit.

"Maximus."

My name on her lips, with that husky quality, has me grinding my cock into the bed. If I hadn't seen the melodious sound come from her directly, I'd think it was a mirage, a fantasy I conjured.

My tongue covers the tiny bud right before I pull it between my teeth. "Say. It." I grit out the words, my own voice gruff now. The vibrations of my mouth on her swollen, overstimulated skin are what finally gets her to acquiesce.

She raises her eyes to the ceiling, and her facial expression, along with her tone, are similar to when one prays. "Please."

The plea is not the begging I originally sought out, but coming from her, it's the equivalent. As a man of my word, I give her what she's asking for, and it's as much for me as it is for her. Maybe even more so.

I suck and lick until her head thrashes, and she lifts her hips to bring them closer to my mouth. There's a moment when she's utterly, eerily still, and then she screams. The pitch and volume of it increase when I thrust my fingers into her and pump them as if they are my cock fucking her.

"Please." This time, her plea is different; it's fearful and full of panic. "I can't."

"You are capable of much, much more, *donnaccia*. Let me show you," I say, caressing her vaginal walls. They constrict around my fingers, and her lips part as her back bows, but there isn't a scream this time. Her orgasm brings about a series of shuddering breaths and staccato moans that punctuate each tremor, each wave of ecstasy, of her coming.

I've never seen anything so fucking perfect in my life.

And it shakes me to my core.

EMILIA

"*G*et up and see to your needs."

I nod at Maximus and get into a sitting position with a muted groan. Every part of me aches, and my muscles scream in protest when I slide to the floor. My feet hit the carpet, and I dig my toes in it to gain purchase as the room tilts momentarily. After shaking my head to clear it, I walk in the direction he indicated. The room is enormous, and I'm not sure I'll be able to make it to the bathroom without tripping, or worse, falling.

Maximus watches me in that way of his, the predatorily sharp gaze roving over every inch of my body. This is most likely the reason he gets to his feet and snatches me into his arms right before I plummet to the floor. He mutters a curse under his breath and carries me over to the toilet before depositing me on the closed lid.

"I'm fine, sir," I say, my face most likely as red as my sore ass.

In answer he quirks a brow. "The last thing I need is you cracking your head on the tile and bleeding to death. So I'm not leaving."

I keep my head bowed the entire time I tend to my personal needs. He's seen every part of me, yet having him hover over me, essentially protecting me, is different. It's...more personal. I inwardly scoff at the idea of him caring for me past anything that has to do with his agenda.

My focus needs to be finding a way to remove myself from it.

He takes my arm and steadies me so I can wash my hands, and for a split second, I lift my head. The image of Maximus and me together stares back. Both of us nude, his darker skin complementing the light shade of mine just as much as his dark hair matches my midnight strands. The green of my eyes is the only splash of color besides the rosiness of my cheeks. When he lifts his hand, I tense and follow it with my gaze, mystified as he traces the curves and twists of a thick lock of hair that covers my breast. He follows the strand to the end, the pads of his fingers lightly skimming my nipple.

The gentle touch confuses me greatly. Maximus spanking me, grabbing me, and choking me are all things I understand, things that have reasons and make sense. But this caress? It doesn't belong in our marriage.

I glance at him from underneath my lashes to get a look at his face only to find his mouth turned down and his brows drawn. His thoughts are hidden from me, as usual, yet this time, he's forgotten to keep his mask of indifference in place.

"Come," he says, pulling me out of my musings. His expression of deep thought is quickly wiped away, almost as if it never existed. And I do the same. He's already learning about me at a rate I find alarming, and I'm not sure how to prevent it further except to say as little as possible.

He assists me back to the bed, and I halt just in front of it, swinging my gaze to his. "Am I to sleep here? I thought..." I stop, my lips slightly parted. His eyes darken, alerting me to his displeasure, and I swallow the nerves creeping up my throat. "I thought I was to sleep elsewhere, sir."

"Is that what you wish?"

My heart sinks in my chest. What is the answer he's looking to hear? I want more than anything to have the solitude that is customary to me, but if I ask for it, will that be the reason he denies me? Or if I say I wish to stay with him, will that make him reject me and give me my secret desire of peace and quiet? There is a third option, and it's the most unlikely one: that he wants me to choose to stay, to choose him. That is outlandish, given how much he hates me, so I discard that right away.

For once, I'm able to hold his gaze, and it's only because I don't see the glimmer of violence lurking in its depths. "The things I wish for are dead and gone," I say, "so the choice of where to sleep is not a choice. You presenting it to me is you offering me the freedom to choose, but we both know it's an illusion. So I choose both and neither, yes and no. Sir."

As though frozen in time, we stay that way while he studies me with an intensity unlike anything I've ever felt from him. It's almost a physical thing, an energy that coats my skin and makes it prickle with awareness. This man, this husband, is turning out to be more complex than I originally thought. At first I assumed his one aspiration was to dole out pain and punishment, and that's something easily done; I know from the times my father hit me. But Maximus? I'm already his captive and bound prey, so there's no reason for him to study that which has already been caught.

Yet he continues to do so, earnestly.

"You're correct," he says. "Your choice, like your opinion, doesn't matter. Get on the bed."

I do as he says and lie on my back, keeping my gaze pointed on the ceiling while my body sinks into the lush bedding. Is this the moment he'll take my virginity? The very thought has panic assailing my nerves, and the muscles along my arms and legs twitch periodically. But as stated before, I don't have a choice in this or anything else.

His footsteps retreat and return a moment later. "Place your hands above your head."

He takes hold of both my wrists and binds them with silk ties. After that he anchors them to the headboard. This should worry me, and my mind tries sending me warning signals, but I ignore them. They'll only frighten me more, making this worse for me.

Fighting one's natural instinct to flee or defend oneself is almost impossible.

Much to my surprise, Maximus leaves the room, shutting the bathroom door behind him. The sound of running water fades to background noise, and with that comes the ability to relax because I'll be alone for at least a few minutes.

I lie there on the soft bedding and let satiation and exhaustion weave their magic over me, causing my lids to lower and a relieved sigh to flow past my lips. Every event with Maximus has been nothing I could've predicted, beginning with our marriage and ending with us gratifying one another. He may think he punished me for my insubordination or subjugated me because I'm Caruso's daughter, but neither is true. The reality is he showed me what ecstasy entails and all the wonders it holds.

Without sex.

The idea of him using his cock to bring me to orgasm is enough to summon mass confusion. I may know his identity, but I don't know the real man underneath the titles of capo, Mr. Silvestri, and husband. There have been no glimpses of the young Maximus I met several years ago, and it makes my heart, the most guarded part of me, ache with sadness and disappointment. I had never thought to see him again after that night, assuming he'd be married by the time I turned eighteen, but when he appeared in my bedroom, all the memories of him flooded my brain and hope swelled in my chest. It didn't take long for him to crush my resurrected dreams, and it wasn't hard for him to do so, since they were quite fragile to begin with.

Nevertheless, marrying the man from my childhood fantasies was never something I thought would happen. And him touching me in such ways? Unfathomable. He's added memories of himself, and I'm not certain I'll be able to shove these aside over time like I did before. Perhaps, but not in the foreseeable future and definitely not when he overwhelms all my senses.

The smell of his cologne, a faint spice, mixed with his natural scent reaches my nose and alerts me to his proximity. The mattress absorbs his weight, and my shivering is barely discernible as he nears me. Then his voice, smoother than the duvet caressing my skin, flows over me.

"Look at me."

I lift my eyelids to find him lying beside me with his head propped up by his hand. "Sir?"

I've learned the consequences of not addressing him properly. His title irks me because of its arrogance, but I like not having to use his name. And I like him not using mine, even more so. The intimacy it would bring would be a farce on so many levels, just as much as him calling me his wife. That title holds nothing for me, offers nothing except a prison.

"You will stay here," he says, his tone leaving no room for interpretation or argument. Maximus is serious about this, and I can't figure out why. "The bindings should keep you in place, but if you attempt to escape them, then I can promise you what happened to you earlier will seem like a delight in comparison. If you thought the handful of swats you received were painful, then just know I'll make it to where the very touch of a breeze will have you gritting your teeth in misery. Am I clear?"

I nod. "Do you wish for me to sleep now, sir?"

He waves a hand with a flick of his wrist. "It doesn't matter to me what you do as long as you stay put."

I nod again and close my eyes in preparation to rest. It tugs at me, and I'm eager to embrace it and leave behind my life for a time, even if it's just in my dreams. The real plans for escape will begin on the morrow. Dawn is already creeping on us, and I'm almost ill with exhaustion. Which means when I feel Maximus's fingers, no more than a whisper against my side, I don't move or stiffen like usual.

He doesn't touch me in any way that's sexual, and after what he's done already, it's nothing inappropriate given I'm his property. However, I want to know why he's doing it to begin with? My aversion to contact with another person is still present, but he has forced it. And not only that; my body is beginning to grow accustomed to the feel of his hands. I used to be scared of touch because my father only did it out of anger through slaps and punches, but after years alone without other humans to interact with? Whatever barrier of fear surrounded me Maximus shattered.

I'm grateful my mind didn't follow suit.

It still could, and any day could be my last. Yet hope has appeared. It is like a single ray of sunshine, easily blocked by the dark sky or thundering clouds, but it appeared the moment he caressed me. That contact, that touch, was different from all the others.

And now I want it.

~

THE ROOM IS FLOODED with light.

I moan softly and turn my face away from the beams of sun piercing my skull. Sleep still lingers, and I mentally brush it away, knowing delaying facing the day won't prevent it from coming. I open my eyes and frown, puzzled by the comforter covering me from the shoulders down. When did that happen? The restraints, although loosened somewhat since last night—or more accurately, earlier this morning—are still in place. Maximus is not present, and relief floods me.

Having him look at me after all the things that transpired between us is not something I want to encounter first thing. Or ever.

I mentally roll my eyes at my childish thoughts, knowing very well I can't avoid him forever. My gratefulness at having this reprieve, a little time of peace to myself, is warranted. I stretch as much as my bonds will allow, and the soreness that greets me in various parts of my body has me frowning. Maximus didn't do any permanent damage to me physically, but my emotional state…well, that's another issue entirely.

How could I enjoy the things he did to me? His hatred of me is abundantly clear, yet by the end of the night, I leaned into his touch and ached for it whenever it left my skin. And not only that, but the pleasure derived from his hands still baffles me as much as the way I responded. Medical textbooks leave much to be desired in the way of true information. There was nothing clinical about what I experienced with my husband.

I harbor no illusions I'm his wife in the true sense, and I wish he'd tell me what his plans for me are. Being locked up again, as opposed to being his plaything to torture, should be preferable. It really should. But I felt alive for the first time in years. To become the sole focus of someone powerful is addictive to me, after having been denied any attention in a long while. I hope it fades, just like I hope Maximus's interest in me dwindles, but what if it doesn't? What if he rewires my brain to the point I'm dependent on him?

Shuddering at the thought, I release a breath. I can't believe he overrode the majority of my abhorrence to physical touch in less than a day. There's a part of me that thinks my subconscious still views him as the young man who called me his sunshine girl.

Ragazza solare.

I remember that moment as if it were yesterday, probably because it was one of the most thrilling days of my life. When I was about eleven years old, Maximus caught me staring at him in the hotel's arboretum after I'd evaded my governess, who was supposed to watch me while my father attended the gala. Maximus and I engaged in a rather unorthodox conversation. Which consisted of me having him promise to marry me someday if no one else wanted to because of my unruly behavior. He agreed, much to my delight, and also escorted me back to my caretaker, who'd filled my head with tales of beautiful men with angelic blood running through their veins. When I grew older, I learned it was the Silvestri family she'd been speaking about.

And he is indeed attractive, more than any man has a right to be.

Is that why I'm drawn to him? After a deep internal assessment, I know it's only part of the reason. I can't fully reject Maximus from my psyche, because I've experienced the good in him. That is what pulls me to him, the glimmer of hope that's still there underneath his hard exterior. He protected me from the kinds of men my father would later on subject me to at the bridal auction, hosted by the Wolf Pack on neutral ground. I never understood why he'd taken me there that night, but I highly suspect it was to upset my mother. She knew I'd be in danger while my father sought out a mistress.

May Alfonso Caruso burn in hell for the things he's done, including the murder of my mother.

Maximus may want to kill him but not more than me.

The door opens, and I jerk up my head as my entire frame tenses. In walks the housekeeper, Rosetta. I didn't catch all of her conversation with Maximus, but their interaction revealed a lot to me. From the way he treated her to the way she spoke candidly to him led me to believe they are very comfortable with each other in a familial way. Also, her usage of Italian makes it obvious that's her original language, and as much as I miss it, I don't want anyone to know I speak it, along with French, fluently. It's the only advantage I have in this situation, and I'm going to keep it secret for as long as I can.

"Good morning," Rosetta says.

"Good morning." My voice cracks, no doubt from a parched throat but also because of my screaming from pleasure last night. The very idea that she, or anyone else in the house, heard me is humiliating. A blush stains my cheeks with heat, and it intensifies when she walks over to untie my bindings.

I peer up at her while she works. Her expression is purely professional and gives nothing away. However, I can't find any disgust or disdain in her caramel gaze. Not that it matters, but it's nice to not receive judgment, especially when I have no say in what's transpired.

"There." She clicks her tongue at the red lines on my wrists, and the wrinkles by her eyes deepen. "I'll give you an ointment after you shower. Come along."

Eager to be clean and wash away any remnants of last night from my body, I shove aside my embarrassment at being nude and slide from the bed. A wave of dizziness swamps me, and I press my fingers to the center of my forehead to be rid of it. My father may have kept me prisoner, but he made sure I was fed in a timely manner, unlike Maximus.

"All the saints above." Rosetta hurries over to me and takes my shoulder to gently set me down on the edge of the bed. Her ire is present in the furrow of her brow and from the thinning of her lips, but it's most prominent in her rapid Italian. "Shit! That boy, for all his intelligence, doesn't use the sense our creator gave him. To leave this poor girl in such a state is a sin against heaven. He better change his ways or I'll tell Father Aldo. His penance won't be as much as I'd prefer, but there's only so much a man of God can do."

If it weren't for the pounding of my head, I'd laugh. That is not what I expected. Well, nothing has been predictable, but her insulting Maximus is by far the least likely thing I would've thought to hear. However, her tone tells me all I need to know: she loves him in a motherly way. And she has a tender heart for her to fuss about my condition, knowing I'm his enemy.

"Relax, *caro*."

Recognition almost flits across my features at the term of endearment. I don't believe she really thinks I'm dear to her like the word implies, but it's still better than *whore*. I use my free arm to cover my breasts to maintain some sort of decency and then tilt my head to appear confused. It doesn't matter because she's already striding in the opposite direction, her steps full of purpose. Within minutes, she returns with a tray of food and sets it beside me.

"Eat slowly and stop just before you feel full," she says in English. Then she hands me a glass of orange juice and two capsules. "Something for your blood sugar and your headache."

Since I didn't see where the medication came from, I only take the juice. She's obviously trying to help me, but I can't make myself take the pills. I down the contents of the glass and sift through my breakfast of eggs, fruit, and toast. Rosetta stands beside me the entire time without rushing me. As strange as it is to have someone in my personal space for an extended period, I find her presence comforting. I think it's because of the way she's fussing over me. It reminds me of my mother, not that it's Rosetta's intent, but I feel it anyway.

"Nothing but water for the remainder of the day," she instructs as she helps me stand. "The color is returning to your face, but your skin still looks pale. You'll be back to normal soon."

Normal. Do I even know what that is? No. Especially not now.

Rosetta rattles off a set of instructions, which consist of me showering, shaving, and brushing my teeth and hair. She has the forethought to set all the essential items on the countertop for me and informs me she'll return shortly and that I'm to be done by then so she can tend to my hair.

"Yes, ma'am," I say.

She chuckles and tucks a stray lock of gray hair behind her ear. "*Caro*, I serve the Silvestri family, and that extends to you now. Please call me Rosetta, not ma'am."

I give her a half smile, which is not much. Then I close the door and purse my lips in thought. She either doesn't truly understand who I am to Maximus, or she doesn't care. I puzzle over this as I shower, but I keep my time short. Just knowing this is where he bathes daily, where he's naked on a consistent basis, is enough to propel me to move quickly. Even so, my mind conjures images of his body, and I squeeze my thighs at the treacherous ache between my legs.

Feeling refreshed after the shower and seeing to my other hygienic needs, I hold up the outfit Rosetta left for me. And then I blink at it. A few times. This can't possibly be meant for me. It's a knee-length deep-wine-colored dress with an elegantly pleated waist and long sleeves. I lightly sweep my fingertips over the soft material and then the diamond earrings right next to it. The only time I ever wore something this nice was when I went to the gala, and that's nothing to reminisce over.

At the sound of footsteps crossing the floor, I hurriedly slip on the dress. It fits like a dream. Rosetta calls out to me and then opens the door only to stop short upon seeing me.

"*Bellissima!*" She claps her hands as though we're two young girls getting ready for prom. Not that I would know what that's like, but I have seen it in movies. Rosetta's delight is infectious, and despite my best efforts, I give her another half smile. "You look better than I imagined," she says. "I'll see to your hair and then give you a tour of the house. Yes?"

I nod and then sit on the footstool she retrieves from inside a nearby closet. Rosetta chatters on about different things while she trims, dries, and styles my hair, and the entire time, I feel like I've entered an alternate universe where the events of the night before never took place. The red lines on my backside say otherwise, and periodically I shift on the seat to alleviate the discomfort. When I walked past the belt lying innocently on the floor earlier, I wasn't sure whether to be upset or enticed. Getting spanked was the last thing I expected to enjoy, and though it stung, the pleasure that came after was incredible.

"Maximus is a very fortunate man to have such a wife," Rosetta says. "Indeed, his brothers will be jealous, but it won't matter because Maximus is the baby of the family and the most protective of his treasures. And you are definitely that. Now come along, *caro*. The tour will take a while if we do it correctly."

I look at myself fully and rise, causing the material to flutter about my knees. I don't recognize the woman before me except for the shining uncertainty in her gaze. That is familiar. But the rest? This can't be me. She's sophisticated yet sensual and...beautiful.

For once, I catch a glimpse of what other people see.

While I wasn't denied clothing, my father only provided the bare minimum when it came to my wardrobe. Not that it mattered to me. In fact, I care very little for material things. They are lovely to have, but knowledge is what I thirst for. However, I can't deny I really like this dress.

"Do you..." I clear my throat and try again at Rosetta's encouraging nod. "Do you think I'll be allowed access to the library or a computer?" My words leave me in a rush, their speed catalyzed by the need to explain my position so I'm not denied the mental escape I desperately need. Learning is my coping mechanism, the only thing that brings me joy in my dreary life. "I want to have something to read, and I don't plan on doing anything I shouldn't. It's just I really like to study and research interesting topics. I won't be in the way, and I'm happy to do it in my room...wherever that is. I promise."

Rosetta places a hand on my shoulder. The touch is light, but I stiffen anyway. I guess I'm not completely over my aversion to touch, and that should apply to Maximus, but the fact it doesn't bothers me.

"I will see to it that you have the things you need, *caro*. Now come along."

This time, I give her a full smile. It's not big, but it's more than before. "Thank you."

She leads us from Maximus's room, and on the way out, my gaze lands on the nightgown I arrived in. It's symbolic in a way. I entered this place full of innocence, and now I'm leaving it without the delicate lace representing my fragility, the youthful hue denoting my naivety, and the length of my gown as a symbol of my sheltered mindset.

I let Emilia sleep in my bed.

I swore I'd never let a woman sleep there, especially not a whore.

Yet sleep there she did, with me beside her, watching her until I fell victim to a restless sleep.

My curses aren't loud, since I have no desire for my brothers to overhear me. They're here to discuss business, particularly an upcoming trip to France, but I know for certain they'll want information concerning my bride. I'm not sure what to tell them either.

What I won't say is I've broken one of my rules. Not only will I never hear the end of it, but then they'll question me and demand an answer.

I don't have one.

Even when I woke to find her nestled, as much as the bindings would allow, in the blanket I'd covered her with, I still couldn't conceive why she was there. Emilia looked like a siren with her raven locks spread across the pillow and her face turned to the side, exposing the graceful slopes of her profile. Her curves weren't fully on display but still able to be seen from the way the sheets hugged her body and clung to her figure. My cock grew hard, and the very thought of it between her rosy lips, parted slightly with her even breaths, was enough to have me ignore my brothers' arrival. Just like I had to jack off in the shower after not taking Emilia's cunt last night, I had to do it again at the sight of her sleeping peacefully this morning.

I walk into my office and find Tristano and Rafael helping themselves to my decanter. Each of them is dressed in expensive clothing; however, Tristano looks every inch the refined businessman he is, complete with a suit and tie. Rafael, on the other hand, wears jeans and a plain gray T-shirt, and his hair is disheveled. He constantly says he doesn't need to be the professional one, since he's not the head of the Silvestri family like Tristano, but I think he'd still rebel and dress in whatever fashion he wanted.

If Tristano is a rule maker, then Rafael is a rule breaker.

And I'm somewhere in the middle, having looked up to both my older brothers my entire life.

"It's about fucking time you showed up," Rafael says. He lifts the tumbler in my direction and raises his brows. "You look like shit, by the way."

I fold my arms and lean against the edge of my desk. "Poor me one and shut the fuck up."

He grins at me while Tristano watches the exchange over the rim of his glass. My eldest brother is always observing and thinking, which makes him dangerous to our enemies.

"Here." Rafael hands me a drink. "So how'd the wedding go?"

I shrug and take a healthy swallow. "As expected."

Rafael groans, and Tristano cocks his head. "And how is that exactly?" he asks. "You need to provide us more details than that."

"That's right," Rafael says with a pinched expression. "You know what this revenge means to us, and not being able to witness Caruso lose his shit when you took his daughter is still something I'm pissed about. The least you can do is tell us everything."

I scrub my face, letting my hand linger before dropping it to my side. "You're right. I wasn't thinking straight, since I didn't get much sleep."

Tristano narrows his gaze and opens his mouth to speak, but Rafael jumps in first. "Did you spend all night fucking that cunt?" My brother's expression turns sly. "I may have missed the wedding, but you could've invited me over for the *reception*."

I exhale, my brain still muddled from lack of sleep but mostly because of Emilia. She's a riddle I can't find the answer to, and it bothers me, which is why I replayed every interaction between us in hopes I'd find some explanations for her behavior. The theory of her being insane no longer holds as much credence as it once did unless she's a glutton for pain, but even then, I saw nothing to indicate that. Overall, I have no wish to speak about her to my brothers until I've discovered her secrets.

"Rafael." Tristano's voice isn't loud, but it doesn't need to be. It's filled with authority, the power of the eldest male and the one our father appointed on his deathbed to lead our family.

My brother is only five years older than me, yet the responsibility he's had to carry matured him quickly. Despite the fact the business was split equally, unheard of in the mafia world and a well-kept secret between us, Rafael and I defer to him.

Tristano is the boss. Rafael is Tristano's adviser, or consigliere. And I am Tristano's second-in-command, or capo. We are a trifecta the criminals of this territory did not see coming.

"Have some respect," Tristano says. "We may despise Caruso, but his daughter is still Maximus's wedded wife. Since our brother sacrificed to marry the girl, the least you can do is let him have his prize." He turns to face me, his gaze sharp. "What I want to know is anything concerning Caruso. I don't give a fuck about his daughter unless she has details of his business dealings and operations. Tell me, Max, how did Caruso react, and does your wife know anything useful?"

I down the contents of my glass and set it on the desk. "Caruso wasn't aware his home was overrun until right before I brought his daughter to him. When I first declared my intention to marry her, he tried to bargain, but when Caruso realized that wasn't an option, he about lost his mind. Losing that alliance with Rossi is not going to sit well with him."

"And the girl?" Rafael asks. "Did she offer any information?"

I shake my head. "I've only had one evening with her, but so far I'm inclined to believe she has no knowledge of his workings. If she does, I'll let you know."

"Perhaps you didn't do your duty as a husband," Rafael says with a grin. "Give the whore to me, and I'll have her screaming and singing like a canary in no time."

Rafael is teasing; it's what he does. This is nothing new, nothing out of the ordinary, but the rage building within me at his joke is far from humorous. In actuality, my fury threatens to spill from me in the form of violence at the thought of my brother fucking my wife. Emilia, with her unspoiled cunt and her throaty moans that rival a siren's call, belongs to me.

And only me.

Tristano, the most observant of us, stares at me with an intensity I find unnerving for once. I quickly smooth over my features as if nothing is amiss and arch a brow at Rafael.

"There is no need," I say, forcing out the words in an even tone. It takes all the self-control I have. "I really don't think she can help us."

When Rafael parts his lips to protest, Tristano cuts him a look that silences him. "Let's move on to the next step in our plans."

I give him a curt nod, relief filling me at the change of topic. "I believe my correspondence with the *Brise de Mer* has gone well. I'm still scheduled to meet with one of their bosses as discussed prior. If we can get this contract, it'll get us one step closer to cutting off Caruso's supply."

Tristano says very little while Rafael and I toss around potential issues as well as expected timelines should this deal go through. Every action we take is with the focus of bringing Caruso to ruin. Each of the seven families repre-sented in the syndicate, also known as the Wolf Pack, specializes in a different type of crime. Caruso is deep into sex trafficking, and for us, it's illegal arms dealing. Not the most profitable when compared to narcotics, but we learned long ago that some avenues of revenue are too costly.

What good is money when your loved one is stolen from you or you're killed?

I always, whether consciously or subconsciously, run my fingers over the tattoo I got in my mother's honor. My brothers and I all did, but though they're located in the same place, they're all different. The centerpiece of mine is a dagger, and on each side of the handle is a small bird, a sparrow representing loyalty. The blade is surrounded by a pair of angel wings that symbolize my mother's transition to heaven, and the birds are my parents. The dagger represents the revenge I'm seeking out on behalf of them both.

Death will come to Caruso, and if there are any others found guilty between now and then, they will be executed as well. When my brothers and I reentered the underworld, it was with new identities, since our father faked our deaths when we were children. I was not more than five or six when it happened, but Tristano remembers everything as if it took place yesterday. He is unusually quiet just like Emilia, and I have a suspicion their odd behavior could be due to the traumas they experienced. After watching Caruso interact with her, and studying my own dealings with Emilia, I have no doubt he was abusive in the physical sense and in the emotional one as well. I have no sympathy, but I'm beginning to understand her.

"Is that everything?" I ask. During the discussion, I kept finding my thoughts straying to the naked woman tied up in my bed. It's understandable because she is beautiful and I can fuck her whenever I please, but it's not conducive to this meeting.

Tristano adjusts his cuff link. "I believe so. Rafael?"

My other brother nods slowly. "Yeah." Then he exhales and groans. "Why does revenge take so fucking long? It's been years since we started this thing, and it could be another year before we finish it."

I share his sentiments, but I have a distraction now, something to keep my mind busy until we're able to ruin Caruso. "Killing him isn't enough," I say. "It's too quick, and he doesn't deserve that."

Rafael rolls his eyes. "You're just saying that because you have a new plaything to fuck around with. I still think you should pass her around so we can all have some measure of revenge. It's only fair."

I take a step forward, unaware I've done so until Tristano grips my shoulder. "Enough, Rafael," he snaps.

My other brother peers at me curiously and then grins. Fuck me. I know that expression.

"So," Rafael says, dragging out the word, "are you leaving Emilia behind when you travel? I'll be a good brother-in-law and *look after* her for you."

He's fucking with me, but that logic doesn't stop me from fuming. "Remove my wife's name from your fucking mouth."

I'm so caught up in my anger I don't immediately spot Emilia and Rosetta standing in the doorway. Before I think to hide my astonishment, I raise my brows at the vision Emilia presents. With part of her hair swept back and piled on top of her head and the rest flowing in loose curls around her shoulders, she is stunning. Her entire body is covered except for her calves, ankles, and forearms, yet the dress hugs her tiny waist, molds to her ample breasts, and flares over the swells of her hips. It showcases everything enticing about her, and my mouth goes dry.

My brothers swivel their heads in her direction, and I grit my teeth to keep from telling them not to. Tristano blinks once, the equivalent of a gasp, and Rafael lets out a low whistle.

"Leave us," I bark at the women.

Rosetta ushers Emilia away, and the second she's out of my brothers' sights, I breathe a little easier. The wrath has yet to subside, but it will. And if not, then I'll unleash the remainder on Emilia for daring to interrupt our meeting.

"Well. Well. Well." Rafael turns to look at me, a smirk on his face and a gleam in his eyes. "I thought you marrying Caruso's daughter might be a hardship. I actually felt bad for you, Max, thinking you were the poor bastard stuck with her. I'm not so sure anymore."

"She is a handsome woman," Tristano says.

Rafael coughs out a laugh. "This isn't the Victorian Era. For fuck's sake, try to speak like you're born in this century." He waves a hand in Tristano's direction. "'She's a handsome woman.' What the fuck does that even mean? She's fuckable, plain and simple."

"She's fuckable by me," I grind out. "And to answer your question, I will be taking her with me to France."

Tristano strokes his chin. "Max, keep me informed at every interval of the negotiations overseas. This is an opportunity we don't want to miss. And Rafael, please shut your fucking mouth before Max kills you. More than enough of our family's blood has been shed, and you two needn't add to it. Loyalty 'til death, my brothers."

Rafael and I repeat the family motto, the one that precedes us from the generations before and one that will continue on long after we're gone.

Tristano gives me a nod in farewell and leaves.

Rafael rolls his eyes, his lazy grin returning. "You know I'm not serious, right?"

I give a minute shrug. "You've always liked to bust my balls. There's not enough maturity in the world to get you to do otherwise."

He chuckles and then punches me playfully in the shoulder. "You're the baby of the family, so it's my duty to toughen you up and make sure you're not a weak-ass bitch."

A reluctant smile spreads my lips. "Your calling from God, I'm sure."

"Yes, among many things." He winks at me. "I'll be off, but if you change your mind about needing a caretaker for your bride, just know I'll do the brotherly thing."

I shake my head and exhale on a laugh. "Loyalty 'til death."

Rafael bows his head in a show of respect. "Loyalty 'til death, brother."

*M*aximus is angry with me. Very angry.

This plays on repeat in my head the entire time I follow Rosetta throughout the luxurious mansion. I don't see it as my home, but it is quite nice. Last night I was too overwrought to take it all in. Today I'm able to somewhat appreciate the expensive tiling, crown molding, grand staircase, and overall decor that's simple but in good taste.

"This is your room," Rosetta says, coming to a stop.

She presses down on the golden handle and opens the door with a flourish. Does it really matter what my prison looks like? No, but I still find myself wondering what Maximus picked out for me. I peek inside, curious despite not wanting to be.

Rosetta waves a hand, beckoning me. "Maximus wanted you to have your own space while he's away on business in France. Don't be shy and come in."

I pull my gaze away from the mahogany bedroom set, and my brows draw close. "He's leaving?"

She pats my cheek in a loving manner that shocks me so much I don't react. "I know you're newlyweds and you'll miss him, but he's not usually gone for more than a couple days, a week at the most."

"A week?" I repeat, disbelief coating my tone.

"Yes, *caro*. I can't believe Maximus is rude enough to leave behind his beautiful bride, but the family business is his life and has been for so long that it'll take a while for things to change." She smiles at me with a mischievous tilt to her lips that makes her look years younger in this moment. "I have no doubt you'll change his mind soon enough. I've seen the way he watches you."

Like he wants to kill me?

It's on the tip of my tongue to utter the thought, but I shrug instead. Luckily for me, a nonverbal answer or acknowledgment is all that's needed to keep Rosetta talking. I like that she doesn't expect me to carry on the conversation or add to it. Instead, she continuously entertains me by expressing almost every thought she has.

Rosetta walks over to the blinds and reaches for the cord to close them. "Like I said before, he won't be gone long, and then you'll be back in his room with him. I'm sure he'll miss you too."

I shake my head. "I can assure you he won't." Is she truly that deluded when it comes to Maximus? I don't want to upset her, but a dose of reality is needed. "This marriage of ours…" I'm not quite sure how to explain what's really happening with me and him. This is anything but a marriage. "Our union was arranged. It was *not* a mutual agreement between him and me."

"Of course it was arranged," she says, putting her hands on her hips. "He is from a very old family who honored the traditions of those before them. Considering the times we live in, some of the crime syndicate members are very stuck in their ways of thinking things ought to be done."

My mouth falls open, and I swing my head around to search for anyone who may have overheard her. She laughs, and the sound is between a wheeze and a chuckle. Before long, Rosetta wipes the tears from her eyes, and I wring my hands, with my gaze darting to the door every so often.

"I've known Maximus since the day he was born," she says. "In fact, I helped bring him into this world. So to answer your unspoken question, yes, I know what the family business entails. Not the specific inner workings but enough to know the Silvestri men are not to be trifled with. They, like all other people from the underworld, where you yourself also come from, value loyalty. I have pledged my life to them and will continue to do so until my last breath. This is why I speak freely."

"Men are quick to demand loyalty, but do they offer it just as quickly?" I mutter.

Rosetta gives me a solemn nod. "It is their way. They're raised with this belief or expectation, and given their lifestyle, it's understandable."

"My family doesn't have a motto. Only the seven families that occupy a seat on the Wolf Pack's council do. Or at least they're the only ones that matter." I shake my head and sigh. "Never mind my ramblings."

Her gaze takes on an analytical feel, and I avert mine to avoid her seeing anything. Rosetta is easy to be around, but I have to remember at all times she is loyal to Maximus and whatever I say will get back to him.

"You do have a motto, Mrs. Silvestri. It's 'loyalty 'til death' because you are part of this family now."

I step closer to the vanity and skim the smooth surface with my fingertips while glancing at myself in the large three-piece mirror. My reflection stares back at me, and I try with all my might to understand what Rosetta sees in me. Why does she treat me like I'm truly respected and viewed as Maximus's wife? It makes no sense, but I don't mind using it to my advantage.

"I'd like to rest for a while," I say. "Will it be difficult for me to procure some reading material or obtain internet access?"

She shakes her head, sending gray strands flying about her face. "I've completely forgotten about that. If you'll give me a moment to organize the kitchen staff for dinner's preparation, then I'll return shortly."

"Thank you."

The second she closes the door behind her, I settle myself on the window seat, reopen the blinds, and stare out. The sun is already setting, which isn't surprising because I was up until almost dawn and slept a large part of the day away. The vibrant colors paint my skin in orange hues and turn the wine color of my dress into a blood red. Ignoring the wrinkling of the expensive material, I tuck my legs and rest my head on the nearby wall that frames the small alcove. I don't want to think about anything. Not where this dress came from, since I doubt it was bought with thoughtfulness or consideration for me. Not why Rosetta treats me so nicely even though her loyalties lie elsewhere. And not why Maximus's touches range from punishing to tender.

The city lights glitter in the distance more so now that the sun has completely set, indicating how much time has passed. I let my imagination, my greatest asset, take me on an adventure. In my mind I'm not associated with the criminal class. Instead, I'm just a regular young woman who attends college full-time. My major is in anthropology, and I'm only in my sophomore year, but I'm on the dean's list due to my excellent grade point average. This night has me dining at an unknown but good-quality restaurant with my...boyfriend.

Maximus's image appears and shatters the fantasy.

With a huff of frustration, I wrap my arms around my knees and place my chin on top. I don't like my husband, the man who forced me into this sham of a marriage, permeating my thoughts. It's bad enough he's taken my body and my freedom, but I want to keep my mind and heart safe. As far as my soul? He's stolen pieces of it.

One for every moan I uttered.

One for every ounce of yearning I felt.

One for every tremor of ecstasy that coursed through me.

Maybe he really is a fallen angel, a demon that owns me in this hell on earth. I quietly recite Our Father as if that will ward off all evil, including Maximus. It's foolish, I know that. If Father Aldo couldn't use the power of God to intervene on my behalf, then I certainly don't have the power to do so. Would Maximus allow me to attend mass or go to confession? It might be the only way I'll ever be able to see the city.

Unless he's the same as my father and plans on keeping me locked away in here.

A knock sounds, and I turn my head in that direction. Rosetta's voice reaches me before I see her, but the first person to enter the room is a young blonde woman who appears to be only a couple years older than me.

"Place the mistress's things over there," Rosetta says. She strides into the room, and there are more tendrils of loose hair bouncing around her face than last time I saw her, giving her a disheveled appearance. "Quickly, Lizbeth. I need you back in the kitchen."

"Yes, signora." She deposits the items on the chaise lounge in the corner. Then Lizbeth gives me a small, timid smile. "Is there anything else I can fetch for you, mistress?"

I shake my head and return the smile. It's awkward on my face, but she doesn't seem to notice. "Thank you."

Lizbeth exits just as fast as she appeared, leaving me alone with Rosetta. "I wasn't sure which books you'd enjoy," she says, "so I took the liberty of bringing you this laptop. Maximus has a newer model and doesn't use this anymore. If you decide to purchase a book, or anything at all, the banking information is already programmed into the computer so you don't need to worry about anything."

My mouth falls open. "Are you—" I stop myself from asking if she's sure this is okay. It doesn't matter if it is or isn't, because I want this. Being without my virtual escape isn't something I know how to handle, and given everything that's happened to me recently, I need it more than ever. "Thank you so much," I whisper, emotion clogging my throat. "I really appreciate it."

I smile, and for once it isn't heavy or fake.

Rosetta returns the facial expression. "Enjoy, *caro*. I'll have your dinner sent up shortly."

I nod, somewhat absentminded, as I snatch up the laptop. I press the gadget to my chest and close my eyes. A sigh of pure contentment flows from me, and soon after, a childlike giddiness spreads from the center of my being. Once again, I arrange myself on the window seat cushion and boot up the laptop. The quality is wonderful, and I can only imagine what the newest version is like. Regardless, the machine does everything I could ever want, and soon I'm diving into a fountain of knowledge and swimming in the data presented. There's no limit to, no discernment of, the topics I choose to study. Usually I follow the trails left by one article that lead to others on similar subjects, just like the crumbs tossed by Hansel and Gretel.

I hope Maximus isn't like a crow and removes my path to information.

The thought of him prompts me to search the country of France, and that's when I lose myself completely. From the historical structures to the culture, it's a place of great intrigue for someone like me. At one point, someone enters the room, and I flick my gaze in their direction to affirm it's not Maximus before returning to the sights offered by Paris. I wonder if he's going there and what he'll be doing. Will he visit any of these wonders and appreciate them as I would? Or is his business trip simply that?

A frown pulls at my lips. What a dreadful existence, if that is the case. I let my inspiration run wild and create a mental list of all the things I'd do if I were able to go. My mouth waters at the cuisine and wines, my nose conjuring the perceived scents, and I briefly close my eyes again to soak it in. Then I let my head fall back against the wall and dream up how magnificent the Eiffel Tower is and how massive the Louvre must be, based on its dimensions. The fabricated voices of the people fill my ears, their beautiful language understood by me.

My ability to speak Italian fluently dwindled once my mother was gone, but during my isolation, I spent months bringing it back to life, in her honor. Once that was complete, I moved on to French and spent several hours every day learning it. I'm not a linguist, but I think I could do quite well if I were to converse with a native French person. This ability adds to my imaginary trip, and I smile to myself as the world I've created pulls me in deeply, submersing me in its excitement and joy.

There have been many freedoms taken from me, but no one will steal my freedom to dream.

MAXIMUS

I take another drink from the crystal tumbler. It goes down smoothly, and the effects of the alcohol spread within me, offering relaxation. It doesn't work.

Nothing about this day has been tranquil.

Several hours have passed since my brothers left, yet embers of anger still burn in my gut. The internal heat flares at the mere thought of Emilia and the vision she presented when she walked past my office. My bride, even with her quirks and unnatural quiet, is exquisite. I've known this from viewing her picture in the past, but seeing her in person is enough to bring any man to his knees.

The way she looked in that dress with her hair styled, along with a splash of cosmetics to enhance her natural beauty, was nothing short of perfection.

And fuck Rafael for looking and admiring.

Well, that among other things. He was also quick to notice my reaction, and not only that, but the motherfucker taunted me with it. Only Tristano was astute enough to intervene. He's always been the most levelheaded in our group, and I don't believe it's because he's the oldest. It's something deeply ingrained in him, and he received it from both our parents.

God rest their souls.

An unbidden, unwelcome thought slips into my mind: What would my mother think of Emilia as my wife? Would she approve of my choice because Emilia has a gentle spirit? Would my mother disapprove of my treatment of Emilia, or is it justifiable due to her connection to Caruso?

It's because of Caruso that I'm not able to ask my mother.

When I was five years old, he gave the Wolf Pack evidence that she was a rat, a person who'd gone to the authorities and divulged the crime syndicate's darkest secrets. The council, in which my father held a seat at the time, was enraged and understandably so. Who would have the audacity to sabotage the members of the underworld? But more importantly, who would dare turn their back on the members of their family? For this reason, my mother was ruthlessly hunted. However, she'd already fled.

Leaving behind a husband and three young sons to reap the aftermath of her actions.

My family was also targeted, not to mention shamed and evicted from the bosom of the world of crime. We lost all our assets, our reputation, and our honor. We almost lost our lives as well. Had our deaths not been faked and our escape kept secret, I'm positive we would've lost them.

Franco, my father, assured us my mother hadn't done anything she'd been accused of. He reminded us day after day, year after year, that she exemplified the family motto of "loyalty 'til death," which meant she was dead because that was how faithful she was.

Thinking of my mother, and the few memories I have of her, is difficult. No one has seen or heard from her in all these years, and my hope of ever doing so dwindles with each day. Logically I know it's highly unlikely she's alive, but as her son, I never want to give in to that notion completely. It's… disloyal to her memory in a way.

"You wanted to see me, Maximus?"

I look up to find Rosetta standing directly in front of my desk. I'm not usually so lost in thought that I don't hear someone approach. It's dangerous to be in that position, and my lack of vigilance has me clenching my teeth. Emilia is fucking with my head, and she's not even trying.

"Yes." I thread my fingers and rest them on the wooden surface. "Why was she let loose?" I don't have to specify the "she." Rosetta became like a mother to me when my family went into hiding, so she knows me better than anyone else. My brothers as well.

"You can't leave her tied up like a dog." Rosetta slaps a hand on her hip and purses her lips. "Eventually the poor girl would've soiled herself and the bed. You may not have to worry about such things, but I do. Besides, she needed to eat and shower."

I squeeze my joined hands to keep from slamming them on the desk. "I recognize that, but when I gave you those instructions, it wasn't for you to parade her around. She isn't a guest here; she's nothing more than a long-term hostage. You know what her father did to the family and how long we've waited to take action."

121

"I know what he did to you, *caro*," she says, her voice taking on a soothing note. "But your wife wasn't born when these events took place. You and your brothers suffered for the perceived sins of your mother, and now you're doing the same to Emilia because of the sins of her father."

My lips part to dole out a scathing rebuttal, and Rosetta raises her voice to speak over me. This stuns me where I sit, anchoring me to the chair. Never has she been blatant in her disrespect.

"You know it's none of my business what you do or how," she says with a narrowed gaze, "but I won't be part of your plans to devastate that poor girl for doing nothing other than being born to an evil man. I'm loyal to this family, no matter what your name is, and I will continue to be. However, I cannot and will not hurt Emilia unless she proves herself to be this culprit you think she is. The Wolf Pack condemned Aida without giving her or your father a chance to prove your mother's innocence, and you despised them for it. Yet here you are, doing the same thing to Emilia without giving her a chance to prove she's nothing like Caruso."

"Are you fucking finished?" I snap.

Her brows lift, and she gives me a curt nod. "Yes, signore."

I'm fuming, and so is she, given her formally addressing me. I don't need to hear her say she's disappointed in me—it's written all over her face—but I can't believe she's defending Emilia to me, knowing who she is and where she comes from. It's unfathomable.

"Where is she now, Rosetta?"

"In the room you assigned her."

Her tone is saturated with disapproval, but I shove that aside. "Anything else I need to know?"

"No, signore."

I wave a hand in dismissal, and Rosetta turns to leave. Although, she makes a point to give me a dirty look, relaying all her unsaid thoughts right before she exits the room. I massage my temples to relieve the pounding there. Bringing Emilia here was supposed to give me satisfaction brought about by her suffering. Yet I have none.

After reopening my laptop and closing out the various documents and internet browser windows, I bring up the camera feed from Emilia's room. I scan the space, and when I don't immediately locate her, my anger flares at the thought of her being gone. But then I find her, curled up underneath the small enclosure in front of the window, her image small due to her compacted position. In order to see her more clearly, I zoom in on her, and the pixels bring her features into focus.

My cock grows hard at the look of pure rapture on her face.

She doesn't make a sound, which perplexes me. The possibility of her being asleep is plausible except for the smile gracing her full lips. I concentrate on that expression, and another current of lust shoots through me. However, it's followed by the realization I've never seen her smile before. Ever.

I think back to the photos I had people take of her, and not one captured the image before me.

For a long while I simply stare at my screen, both confounded and entranced. Her not showing joy in my presence isn't a mystery because I know I've given her nothing to be happy about. And I assume the same of Caruso. Not that I enjoy being put into the same category as him, even for benign reasons such as this. After watching Rosetta all these years, I've learned women are emotionally resilient. Surely this can't be the only time Emilia has been like this? Which leads me to the next logical thought: What brought this about?

My fingers fly over my keyboard until I have the answer. Every click of the mouse, stroke of the keys, and website visited sits in front of me in a collection of data. I sift through it, knowing there's nothing threatening within. If there were, I would've been alerted. Originally, I hadn't planned on giving her the laptop, but after learning nothing important about Caruso's business dealings, I devised a plan. Giving Emilia that computer will accomplish several things. It will show me if she tries to contact her father, which could prove their relationship isn't as distant as I was led to believe. She might even go as far as to report things back to him. The correspondence would be intercepted and shut down before it was delivered, but she wouldn't know unless I told her. Secondly, anything she researches could give me a clue to something I may have missed. And lastly, her activity will give me a direct view into her mind.

And what I discover is mundane.

It's France, specifically Paris, and everything tourists generally do when visiting that location. Rosetta must've told her of my upcoming trip, but why would that prompt Emilia to extensively research this? Does she know something about *Le Milieu*, the crime syndicate in France? If so, then there's nothing on my screen to indicate that. Does she think to go with me, as if it is a vacation? I doubt that. She doesn't want to be around me, let alone do frivolous things such as the events listed before me.

Having found nothing nefarious, or significant, I close it all out and bring her up on my screen again. Emilia's wistful expression is still present. I study it extensively until I end up with more questions than answers percolating in my mind.

Eventually, I shove back from the desk with a grunt of frustration and slam the laptop closed. Leaning back in my chair, I steeple my fingers and rest my chin on them, slipping deep into thought. Rafael taunted me about watching over my bride while I was gone, and this prompted me to foolishly announce I'd be taking her with me to France. Except, it wasn't only Rafael's jibe that persuaded me to act rashly.

It was the extreme interest and attraction that flared in both my brothers' eyes when she appeared.

Tristano's disappeared quickly out of respect for me and her. He's always been the honorable one, the gentleman. But Rafael's gaze ignited with lust, and this provoked me severely. He couldn't hide it, and I'm not sure he wanted to. Goading me, along with everyone else, is a favorite pastime of his. And he found the perfect weakness to exploit and send me into an irrational jealousy.

I've avoided fucking Emilia, because I wanted the fear of that threat looming over her at all times. I wanted her to constantly fret over the prospect of me taking her body, under my terms and on my timeline, but all that changed the second I touched her cunt and found it drenched with arousal.

That fucked me up like nothing I've experienced.

Since then I've kept from fucking Emilia, because I don't trust myself. I enjoyed watching fear brighten her green eyes and hearing her sharp intake of breath at the feel of my fingers on her skin. I delighted in the expression that crossed her face when she attempted to hold back her orgasm. And her full lips hungrily sucking my cock? I about fucking died from pleasure. Those things, plus a good number of others, lead me to believe I'll lose myself in her body.

Ultimately forgetting her identity and mine.

With a string of curses, I open the laptop and retrieve the camera feed of her room again. She doesn't have that faraway look anymore, but the smile is still present. It's less than before, yet her attractiveness hasn't waned. If anything, seeing her this way has made it grow.

There's a knock on Emilia's door, and a simple keystroke reveals Rosetta just outside. She enters Emilia's room with a tray in hand, her voice easily carrying to the speakers and therefore to me.

"My old bones scream seeing you in that position." She sets down her burden on the vanity and massages her lower back with both hands. "Have you been sitting there all evening?"

Emilia's face takes on a sheepish expression, her eyes downcast when she shrugs.

"You need to eat," Rosetta says. She wags a finger in the younger woman's direction. "If you don't, I'll take the computer away."

"I'll eat."

Rosetta crosses her arms, and although her back is facing me, I know what type of look she's giving Emilia. The corners of my mouth twitch at the speed at which my bride closes the laptop and hops down from her perched location. She gracefully lowers herself onto the vanity chair and takes a bite, her gaze never leaving the housekeeper.

"Very good," Rosetta says. "Will that be enough for you?" Emilia nods, and then Rosetta asks, "What about dessert, *caro?*"

The fork halts midway to Emilia's mouth. "Is that permissible?"

Rosetta cackles and grins. "Of course, unless you request something outrageous that will take the chef too long to prepare in a timely manner. What would you like?"

I lean forward, stupidly curious about what she might choose. Caruso may not be as wealthy as my brothers and me, but he is a far cry from being destitute, yet at the mention of a dessert, Emilia's entire demeanor changed. It was subtle. However, I'm rapidly learning to interpret her body language as well as translate her nonverbal responses.

"Would it be too much to ask for cheesecake?" Emilia's voice is low, barely above a whisper. I shift closer, but if I get any more so, I'll hit my head on the screen.

Rosetta shakes her head, and Emilia's face falls. "That won't be hard at all."

The elation that lights up my bride's eyes catapults me into a memory from long ago, to a time when I stared into a similar gaze made up of brilliant emeralds that captivated me as no woman's has until now. My breathing halts in my lungs when I conjure the image of the young girl's face. I nicknamed her *ragazza solare*, sunshine girl, because of the unadulterated joy that emanated from her. She was at the first gala I was forced to attend because if someone didn't, it was considered an insult to the Wolf Pack, and that's an invitation for retribution. It was the young girl's presence that helped me make it through the night. Comparing the ages of her and

Emilia, as well as their features, it's entirely possible they are one and the same.

I immediately dismiss the thought. *Ragazza solare* had a pure soul, kind heart, and audacious demeanor, and my bride carries none of these traits. She may have the same dark hair and green eyes, but that could be mere coincidence. I can't believe I entertained the idea they are one and the same, which is an insult to the young girl who ordered me to marry her. Whenever I've replayed our interaction over the years, it's never failed to wipe away some of the darkness that stains my soul.

If I were to meet her as a grown woman, I wouldn't approach her, because the darkness in me is like ash and soot, dirtying and ruining everything it comes into contact with. But I would look at her, and my curiosity—concerning what had become of her—would be satisfied.

Rosetta walks across the room to exit, and her movement draws my gaze back to the screen and my mind to the present. Emilia clears her throat, and the housekeeper turns to face her.

"Thank you," Emilia says. She smiles, and it dazzles me just as it did a few moments ago. "You've been kind, and I just... thank you."

"You're welcome."

I continue watching my bride, who grabs the laptop as soon as the door shuts. She doesn't hesitate to reoccupy the location by the window, curling her legs underneath her tiny frame. The light from the screen flickers over the fragile contours of her face, and her fingers are a blur. My curiosity rises to the forefront again, and I curse myself while I go to view what she's looking at.

Pont des Arts, the love lock bridge.

That's a place where couples go with the intention of placing a metal lock, sometimes with their names on it, on the bridge's railing or grate. Emilia doesn't have a boyfriend or fiancé, so there's no reason for her to search this when there are so many other famous sites in Paris. So why is she?

Although Emilia obviously doesn't have a fiancé, she did at one point. Rossi. Has she lied about her relationship with him? Is this a place they talked about going together in the future or perhaps for their honeymoon? Is she thinking about him right now, in my fucking house?

Every thought and question is like kindling for the fire building within me. I'm on my feet and climbing the grand staircase before I've thought about why I'm enraged. I don't tolerate liars, but there's more to this than simple deception. Knowing what I do about Rossi, I doubt he cares for her. However, he could try to steal her from me. Another idea is Emilia has feelings for him.

If she's a slave to anyone emotionally, it's going to be me.

I don't knock but manage to keep from slamming the door when I barge in. Emilia gives a startled cry, and her eyes become perfectly round with shock. The element of surprise should never be underestimated, which is why I resent her for ambushing me several times with her quirks and profound words.

"What are you doing?" I ask, my voice deadly quiet. It's a complete contrast to the loud pounding in my blood.

Emilia sets down the computer as though it's a snake and wrings her hands. "Visiting harmless websites for entertainment."

I shut the door behind me, and when the mechanism clicks, she winces. I assume an air of nonchalance and lean against the wall, crossing my arms. "What websites?"

She's taking a test, one that will be graded by me and where there is only one right answer: the truth.

"Anything that has to do with common tourist attractions in Paris."

She averts her gaze, and I narrow mine. "Look at me," I say. After she obeys, I continue on. "Tell me why."

"Rosetta told me you were leaving for France, and I've never been there, so I was curious."

Emilia lowers her head as a blush sweeps over her cheeks, and then she brings her gaze back to me. Smart of her. My palms itch with the need to smack her ass until it matches her face in color, although she's done nothing wrong. Seeing as she's my property, there's no reason I can't punish her, but Rosetta's words come back to haunt me.

My mother wouldn't approve of me treating an innocent woman this way.

Emilia picks up the device and holds it out with the screen in my direction. "You can see for yourself. I have nothing to gain by lying."

But does she have something to lose by telling the truth?

"Do you know if Caruso has any business connections in France?" I ask. "Or Rossi?"

She shakes her head, and the drop earrings with diamonds catch the light, sparkling as they glide to and fro along the slope of her neck. After Emilia sets down the computer, she pulls her bottom lip between her teeth, and I mentally groan. Why does she do provocative shit all the time?

I narrow my gaze, shoving aside the beginnings of arousal. "If I find out you know something, you'll regret it."

"What do you think I'll do with that information?" She wraps her arms around her legs and seems to shrink before my eyes, folding into herself. "I have no access to my father's accounts and no money of my own, so why would I help him? He was horrible to my mother and me, and while you've put me through a lot, you'll never be worse than him."

I was suspicious that Caruso didn't treat Emilia well, but hearing it doesn't bring me an emotional reward. If anything, I'm dissatisfied. Perhaps even disconcerted.

"Sir, I would rather be tied to your bed than free to roam my father's house, because I hate him." She says this quietly; however, her voice is dense with fury and pain. A lot of it. This holds me captive, as does the fiery green of her eyes. "Believe the worst and do your worst, because you can't take from me more than he already has. Life isn't a competition, but I may want him dead more than you."

We stare at one another until she ducks her head and rests her chin on her knees. Emilia looks so vulnerable and delicate sitting there, yet she just revealed how much she loathes her father, the very man I despise with my entire being. There are commonalities between her and me that are to be expected, seeing as we come from the same world. But I can't wrap my mind around the idea she wants Caruso to die.

Emilia is still my enemy. However, the enemy of my enemy is my friend. That's how the saying goes anyway. What does this mean for her and me?

I push away from the wall. "Come here."

She flicks her gaze to me and then away. I wish she would stop doing that so I could read her expression more easily. Emilia isn't exactly an open book, and I think whatever emotions I do catch on her face are only a small representation of the thoughts in her mind.

As she makes her way to me, I peruse her body, starting with the gentle but provocative sway of her hips, to the flush scattered across her breasts, and ending with the blue-black tendrils framing her face. Her beauty entices me, of that I have no doubt. But I'm finding out there's more to this woman than I could have foreseen.

She stops an arm's length from me and lifts her head enough for our gazes to meet. Acceptance is in hers. Usually there's fear clouding the green hue of her eyes, and although there is some, it's not as much as I expected. It's lessened, but so has my anticipation at seeing her frightened.

Have I replaced the desire to torment her with something else?

Impossible.

EMILIA

*M*aximus stares at me for so long I think he's never going to speak. During this time, I mull over everything I said, and it has me pressing my lips together. It was so stupid of me to challenge him by saying he couldn't hurt me more than my father already has. It's the truth, but I didn't need to tell him. Will Maximus make more of an effort to ensure I'm miserable?

Well, more than I am now anyway. And that's not too bad, all things considered. Yes, my husband has used me, but I didn't expect anything less. Actually, I expected things to be far worse, and surprisingly, he does treat me like a human being on occasion. If I could figure out how to ensure that happens more often, I'd be fortunate. In time, when he grows tired of using me for his personal gains, I could even be happy. Maybe. Rosetta is kind to me, and the household staff didn't look at me with contempt, which means my only obstacle in having a decent life is Maximus.

From the way he pierces me with his gaze, I know I won't have a peaceful existence anytime soon.

"Do you really hate Caruso that much?" he asks.

"I do."

"Why?" The confusion in his tone is genuine. "He's your family."

"He's a murderer."

I can't and I won't say anything more about that, even if Maximus beats me for it. My mother is not something I'll share with anyone but him especially because he doesn't deserve it. And I'm sure he feels the same about me when it comes to his revenge. If Maximus wants me to know why he hates my father, he'll tell me.

If not, I hate Caruso enough for both of us.

Maximus cocks his head, and a strand of midnight hair falls across his brow. "And what do you think of Rossi?"

I blink and rapidly gather my thoughts at the unexpected question. I've never liked Rossi, and the first time I met him, I couldn't wait to get away. He didn't do more than kiss my hand, but he reeked of licentiousness, and it soured my stomach. The way he looked at me was with more than attraction; it was filthy and very unlike the way Maximus watches me.

I'm not sure if it's the flaring of his nostrils or something else that tips me off, but when Maximus grabs my upper arms, I'm able to keep from crying out in surprise. He yanks me to him and lifts me off the floor until I'm on my toes and his face is a breath away from mine. This close I'm able to make out the churning in his dark eyes, which look almost fevered.

"You better answer me right the fuck now," he bites out between clenched teeth, "or God help me, I'll whip your ass raw. Do you have feelings for Rossi?"

My mind goes blank.

For the first time in my life, I've forgotten how to articulate a sentence or express a coherent thought. And all because Maximus sounds like a jealous husband. I know he's not, that he hates me almost as much as my father, and yet... Why does he care?

I don't realize I've spoken aloud until Maximus repeats the question.

"Why do I care?" As he asks me this, his voice rises in volume, and I wince at the ferocity of it. I've never witnessed him out of control, but right now it looks as though he's about to become unhinged. My body trembles from nerves and excitement. His behavior means something, and I've gone too far to turn back from the truth.

I hope the price I'm willing to pay is worth it, because Maximus will collect on that debt. And soon.

"Yes, sir," I say. "I mean nothing to you, so you shouldn't care whether I have feelings for Rossi." I pause to stem a grimace due to him squeezing my arms tighter. I can't tell if it's on purpose or not. "So my feelings for someone else are inconsequential."

With a sound that's something between a growl and a roar, Maximus snatches me off the floor. I land on his shoulder, and a puff of air shoots from my mouth when my stomach slams into the muscles there. Then I'm sucking in a breath the second after his hand connects with my ass. It stings badly, and I wriggle in his hold while trying to gain purchase by gripping his shirt. My head bobs as he walks, his steps angry and quick, and my hair blocks my side view, but I'm able to recognize his bedroom once he enters it. The door closes with a bang, and I flinch.

He wraps his hands around my hips only to toss me onto his bed. I land on the mattress, stunned for a moment, and then shove my hair from my face. Maximus is on me faster than I can draw breath, and the length of his hardened body crushes mine into the duvet. Even fully clothed, I can feel every part of him as my curves mold to fit him, to welcome him.

"S-sir," I manage, my gaze pleading. "I'm—"

My words disappear when he roughly grips my jaw. "Not another fucking word."

He doesn't give me time to agree or disagree. With a jerk, he turns my head to the side and brings his mouth to my neck only to press his teeth onto my skin. I cry out, and my hips lift, straining underneath his weight. My mind shuts down completely and sends a massive adrenaline surge through me to aid in my escape.

But Maximus isn't letting me go anywhere.

I throw out my arms and dig my nails into the meat of his biceps, trying to keep him at bay. Or is it to steady myself because I'm careening into a chasm of lust? It doesn't matter when he leans into me to snatch both my wrists. With a hard jerk, he extends them above my head, pinning them down with one hand. My breathing is erratic, and my breasts press against his chest, my nipples rubbing with every inhale.

Maximus bends down his head and licks the spot he just bit and then moves up an inch to do it again. This bite isn't as painful as the first, although I still shiver, unable to help it. I'm always at his mercy, but this is different. *He* is different. I crossed a line, said something I shouldn't have, and now he's teetering on the edge of his control.

Or maybe his control has snapped and I'm about to feel the consequence of it.

"Maximus," I whisper.

He lifts his head to stare at me and once again he grabs my jaw, keeping me from looking away. "That is the first of many times you'll say my name. And the next one will be on a scream." Though his voice sounds calm, he can't hide the tumultuous emotions within his gaze.

Will my scream be of pain or pleasure?

Maximus lowers his hand, and I let my head fall to the side when he goes back to skimming the length of my neck with his lips. I prepare for his bite, and it comes. On my nipple. Even through my clothes, it's enough to have me cry out, and the sensitive peaks harden more. As though triggered by the sound, Maximus grinds his cock into the apex of my thighs, and it spreads my legs but not fast enough. With his fingers gripping the backs of my knees, he wrenches my legs apart, and a whimper escapes me at the forceful action.

Then he snakes his hand underneath my dress to cup my sex. I squeeze my eyes shut and wait, my entire frame shaking, half from anticipation and the other anxiety. Not knowing what to expect is what frightens me about him, but what I do know is that Maximus has awakened me, both physically and emotionally.

And now I can't turn it off.

There's not a single part of my body that doesn't yearn for him to touch it, and I lie there praying he will, even if it comes with his fury. From men, the only physical contact I've experienced has originated from anger, and Maximus is no different; he's just made it more pleasurable than painful, further warping my expectations of touch.

His ragged breaths skim my ear. "Whose cunt is this?"

"Yours." This truth is easy to admit.

He presses his thumb onto my clit, making me gasp as sensation zips along my nerves, and my sex dampens more. All thought evaporates in the blaze of arousal torching me. I'm on fire, and with every circular motion of his thumb, I get that much closer to combustion. All the while, he nips at the shell of my ear and runs his tongue down my neck.

His hot breaths flow over the sensitive area, pushing me to the edge. "Tell me about Rossi."

My response is a groan because he shoves my panties aside and thrusts two fingers inside me. My sex clenches around him, and the only thing I can think about is finding relief in my orgasm.

"*Donnaccia*, I'm getting impatient." Maximus withdraws his hand only to shove his fingers in again but with more power this time. He does this over and over, and though I can hardly move with him on top of me and with my arms restrained, I arch my back, letting my head rest on the pillow.

"What do you want to know?" I say with great effort.

Maximus sucks on the side of my neck directly over my pulse, which is running wild. "What do you feel for him? Tell me or I'll force it out of you." He moves to the hollow of my throat and flicks his tongue over the area as if wanting to absorb my answer.

"Nothing." I gulp for air and struggle to shape it into words. "I feel nothing for him."

He freezes, his fingers inside me and his cock pulsing against my thigh. "Open your eyes." When I do, he continues with a command that makes my sex spasm. "Say. It. Again."

Through a haze of intense lust, I gaze up at him in total surrender. "He means nothing."

Maximus's entire countenance shifts, almost like a veneer has been lifted from him. The glowing in his eyes morphs from rage to vindication, but it's no less dangerous.

Or provocative.

He returns to stroking me, and within seconds, I'm twisting in his hold, bombarded with sensation. "Say my name." His voice is low yet powerful. My skin prickles at the raw energy pouring from him and coating his words. I open my mouth to give him what he wants, and nothing comes out except another moan. He's rendered me incapable of speech or anything else except feeling.

"Fucking say it," he grits out. His impatience swells, as does my orgasm, and that sends me over.

A scream is ripped from my throat when pure ecstasy hits me, and somehow I'm able to articulate every syllable in his name. It steals everything I have. Before, my body was taut with the need for release, and now it undulates under the natural rhythm of pleasure spreading through every part of me. When it begins to subside, I slowly fall back into a more corporeal state of consciousness with the remnants of the orgasm causing my body to gently shake.

Maximus lets go of my wrists and withdraws his hand from my sex only to grab the hem of my dress and push it to my waist. He grips my panties and all but rips them from my body, tossing them to the floor. I bring my arms to my chest, as though to protect myself, but I never take my gaze off him. He undoes his belt and pants to free his cock, taking it in his palm to stroke it. His eyes drop to between my legs, and his gaze flashes.

My predator has found a mate.

He lowers himself until the weight of him traps my arms between our bodies. With one arm used to stay propped up, he positions his cock at my entrance, and I slam my eyes closed, turning my head.

"Look at me." Maximus cups my cheek and brings my gaze back to him. "In this bed and in this marriage, there will be no one else but me. Every memory and fantasy you've ever had will be erased because I will fuck them out of you until you can't speak any name but mine."

He eases into me, and his hand on my face trembles. I stare up at him, watching his pupils contract and the tendons strain in his neck. I note the thrumming of his heart against me, matching my own, and the way his movement is completely controlled. My breaths stop at the feel of him slowly claiming my body with every part of him that fills me. When he withdraws, I blink up at him, not understanding until he enters me fully with a single thrust.

"I fucking own you," he says on a groan.

Then he proves it.

Maximus enters my body, pistoning into me, and every thrust is more severe and deeper than the last. I'm no longer able to hold back the moans that flood my mouth and spill over my lips, and every time I utter a sound, he rubs my lower lip with his thumb. My sex fists his cock, making it slick with my cum, and he drives into me with a ferocity that borders on madness.

And I savor it. His insanity now matches mine.

He raises one of my arms and guides it to wrap around his neck. That's when I know I'm not alone in this emotional vulnerability I'm feeling. I cling to him, matching the movements of his body to meet every gyration of his hips with my own. His groans reverberate in my ears, and I reciprocate by whispering in his. With every stroke of his cock, I say his name, giving him what he wants. Because he's giving me what I want, which is human connection.

His cock swells inside me, and I don't have to be told what to do. I keen his name, my voice getting louder when Maximus reaches down to rub my clit. I come, and he follows me into bliss.

Maximus leans on his forearms and lets his head hang while his chest heaves with breath. I've never been permitted to touch him, and the daze I'm in emboldens me, so I run my fingers through the hair at the nape of his neck. He jerks up his head to pierce me with his gaze, and I jolt right before bringing my arms down and tucking them to my chest. We stare at one another, him pulsing inside me and me clenching his cock, and for once his gaze isn't shuttered. In the beautiful onyx of his eyes, there's a sense of awe mixed with disbelief that resonates with me because that's what I'm experiencing looking at him right now.

With agonizing slowness, he lowers his head, and I drop my gaze to his lips. Right before his mouth touches mine, he opens it and takes my bottom lip between his teeth. He watches me gasp when he sucks and licks, running his tongue over the places I broke the skin from biting it. With one hard pull of his mouth, a small stream of my blood flows to him. A tiny smear coats his lips, and I squirm underneath him, arousal striking me at the visual. And I'm not the only one. Maximus's cock hardens, causing my eyes to widen.

"Why did you do that?" I ask, my voice barely audible.

"I have your innocence and now your blood." He withdraws from me and sinks back into me with a loud exhale. "No one can take them from me. They are mine, and so are you."

This time his movements, although still controlled, are languid and tantalizing. Maximus watches my face as passion overtakes me, and when I'm lost in him, he slides his hand in my hair, using the grip to slowly force my head back. With my neck fully exposed, he places an openmouthed kiss just under my jaw. The act is sensual but soft and so shocking. He does it again over the bite mark from earlier, and in an almost apologetic way, he glides his lips over the area. I might be in a state of euphoria, but I know I'm not imagining the difference in him.

Maximus brings about my orgasm, and the intensity of it, paired with this tender side of him, has emotion gathering in my chest. On impulse, I throw my arms around his neck, and he releases my hair, leaving me to bury my face against the slope of this throat. Then he slides an arm along my back to splay his fingers in a firm hold, pressing my body to his. I grip him tighter, and the moment I come, I bite him, wanting to be as close as possible but also excite him like he did me.

"Fuck!" he rasps.

His orgasm hits him, and he thrusts into me until he's spent. In this moment, I've never felt closer to someone, more vulnerable, and more scared in my life. Having one's body laid bare is entirely different from having one's soul exposed this way.

I give a tiny shriek when he rolls and reverses our positions, leaving me sprawled on top of him. My cheek lies directly over his heart, and I focus on the steady cadence to keep from spiraling in my mind. This is sex, a physical need that's been met. Nothing more.

I'm not very good at lying to myself with his cock in me.

Sex with Maximus is something I didn't know I wanted, and now it's something I don't want to go without. Will he discard me, since my innocence is gone? Will he get his sexual gratification elsewhere from now on?

The feel of his fingertips tracing the length of my spine has me stiffening.

"What are you thinking?" His voice is lazy with threads of contentment. And it's so unlike him. "Tell me."

I hurriedly grasp at any notion that could explain my reaction. When my gaze lands on the bed frame, I blurt out an answer. "I'm wondering where I'm going to sleep tonight, and if it's my room, do I have to be tied up or not?"

He stops the gentle caress on my lower back. "Where do you want to sleep?"

With you.

I press my lips together to keep from saying that thought aloud. Maximus doesn't want me here with him, and I shouldn't want it either. Yet the feel of our bodies flush, connected in a way that goes beyond words, is something I don't want to end.

"Anywhere that doesn't require me to be tied up," I say.

There's a small lilt in his voice when he speaks; maybe it's even the hint of a forthcoming smile. "I can understand that."

I scoff. "I doubt you've ever been secured to someone's headboard."

"No, I can't say I have."

There's definitely amusement coating his tone, making him sound more carefree than I've ever heard him. It's...nice. What does he look like when he's like this? I take a chance to find out and lift my head to see his lips tilted in a smirk. My heart thunders in my chest.

"Well," I say with a sigh, "take it from me when I say it's not a comfortable way to sleep."

He nods as though in slow motion, but he's no longer with me; mentally he's elsewhere. I wish I could follow him and discover his hidden thoughts, the ones he doesn't share with anyone, maybe not even himself. Human beings are complex creatures, and our subconsciouses aren't always brought to the forefronts of our minds. With Maximus, I sense layers of buried emotions he has yet to acknowledge or even experience. And I'm sure the same could be said about me.

"Come on," he says. "Get up."

His command shatters the serenity of the moment, and I'm quick to leave the bed but not only that; I have to leave what transpired between us there too. I can't take that intimate time with me unless I want it to destroy the walls I've built to protect myself.

I make my way around the bed and head toward the door, eager to escape. There's a bathroom connected to my room, so that's my destination. I need to wash Maximus from my body. And mind, if possible.

I'm so caught up in my objective I jump when the door slams in my face. Maximus removes his hands from the wood to plant them on my shoulders and spins me to face him. After that he positions his palms on either side of my head, caging me, and I stare up at the scowl on his face.

"Where the fuck do you think you're going?" he asks.

"To my room. I thought you were done with me."

His eyes narrow to little more than slits. "Did I tell you to leave?" I shake my head and then suck in a breath when he puts his knee between my legs, parting them. "You have my cum running down your thighs, my marks on your neck, and my sweat on your body, so you're not going anywhere."

He peels himself from me, straightens to clamp a hand on my wrist, and leads me to the bathroom. Once there, he takes my chin, and my gaze darts to his. "Don't move."

I nod and then wait. In the time I stand there, self-conscious from everything that's transpired, Maximus removes his clothes, turns on the shower, and then returns to me. I reach for my zipper, and he arches a brow until I drop my hand. Like I'm fragile, he takes off my dress, stopping to stare at the stain on the material. He swings his gaze to me, and the possessiveness within has my lungs collapsing. It's gone in a wink, and then once I've removed my bra, he's guiding me into the shower.

With my bottom lip between my teeth, I stand there without an inkling of what he wants me to do. Until he tells me to wash him. My hands tremble the entire time, and not once do I look him in the eyes. He's gorgeous, sin made flesh.

Maximus doesn't utter a word when I tend to him, and I'm relieved as soon as I'm done. I find that touching him would be enjoyable if it were initiated by me, not ordered by him. But when he touches me? I have yet to truly hate it.

"Don't ever cut your hair."

His voice breaks through my thoughts. "Okay."

He takes a wet strand and tucks it behind my ear. "I mean it. You can get it trimmed, but I'll be pissed off if you cut it. Now turn around."

I sway out of pure rapture when he begins to wash my hair. He steadies me, muttering under his breath, but I don't hear him. All I can concentrate on is how glorious this feels. Maximus cleans my hair and my body, and by the time the shower is done, I'm an emotional mess. What he did to me was just as intimate as, if not more than, sex to me.

In a daze, I watch him drag a towel over every inch of my skin and then hand me a large shirt. The scent of him reaches my nose, and I inhale deep while getting dressed. Once again, Maximus, now wearing nothing but shorts, takes my wrist and tugs me toward the bed. With a resigned sigh, I crawl onto the mattress and position myself where the ties should go, staring up at the ceiling while willing myself not to show emotion. Disappointment tugs at me, and I don't want to examine why. Did I really think sex would change things between us?

There's innocence, and then there's ignorance.

Maximus gets into the bed, and I brace myself, already feeling the pressure of the restraints. "Would you like me to be under the covers first, sir?"

"I'm not tying you up."

I swing my gaze from the ceiling to him, unable to keep my expression blank. "You're not?"

He shakes his head, and I lie there stunned. The change I sensed is not an illusion. And I don't know how to handle it or how to act. So I revert back to what I'm familiar with.

"Do you want me to stay outside the covers?" I ask.

He shrugs, and it contrasts with the tight set of his shoulders. "It's your choice."

Without a word, I slip under the sheets and then go back to staring into nothingness, hoping my mind makes sense of all this. I don't know what I'm waiting for exactly. Maybe I think he'll change his mind, or maybe this is just another one of his games. It's hard to say, since I can't understand the motives for his behavior. Like caring for me after sex? I wouldn't have thought that a possibility in a million years let alone tonight. So what prompted him? Guilt is the only answer I can come up with, and even that doesn't resonate fully.

He turns off the lights in the room with the remote on his nightstand and then faces me. "If you leave this bed without asking me for permission, I'll assume it's with the intention to take my gun and shoot me. Are we clear?"

I glance at him. "Yes."

Darkness eats up most of the room, and my ears quickly become attuned to the subtle noises drifting about. The one that has my attention is Maximus's breathing. It's slow and even, and I listen to it for a long while, waiting for sleep to overtake me. That's why I readily pick up the sound of him shifting on the mattress. What I don't expect is for him to grab me.

My strangled cry hits the air when Maximus snakes an arm across my middle and pulls me to him. He tucks me to the length of his body, looming over me with his head propped on his hand, his hair askew and draped over his cheeks.

"Relax," he whispers, the low vibrations transferring to me where we touch.

I stare up at him with wide eyes, somewhat able to make out his features in the dark. My heart races, and I lie pressed up against him, stiff as a board. He glides his thumb back and forth over the smooth expanse of my stomach, just below my ribs. No more words are given and none received, yet an unspoken message travels between us as he lies back down and adjusts me so that my back is flush to his chest. I bite my lip at the feel of his semihard cock, waiting for him to take me again.

Instead Maximus wraps his arm around me, anchoring me in place, and then buries his face in my hair. He inhales deep, and the tip of his nose follows the back of my neck until his mouth is at the curve where my neck meets my shoulder. His lips graze the skin there, and I swallow the sigh in my throat. Was that a kiss? A show of affection?

"Keeping you like this will dissuade you from making a choice that could get you killed," he says. "That's why I have you in this hold."

I'd believe that if he didn't tighten his grip on me and nuzzle the side of my neck before drifting to sleep, his hand resting on the area directly above my heart.

A breath of air stirs my lashes, and my eyes flutter open.

The disorientation of sleep surrounds me like a fog, and the warmth seeping into me threatens to pull me under the lull of repose once more. I glance down to find the source of the heat: Maximus's arm draped across my chest, his palm covering one of my breasts. He releases another breath, and the tiny current grazes my face.

With great care and slowness, I turn to look at him, and my heart leaps at the sight. The hard lines usually present around his eyes and mouth are gone, giving him a more relaxed expression. Without the ever-present tension and anger, he's less a fallen angel and more a man—a human who is far from perfect but still clings to redemption.

Waking up in his bed this way cannot be any more opposite to the last time.

Yesterday I was a literal prisoner, tied to the bed after being used for his pleasure, which inadvertently brought about my own.

Today…I'm being held prisoner in a display of possession but without negative connotation. And last night I was given pleasure, not used for it.

Yesterday I was a mistress, and today I feel like a wife.

The dynamic has shifted, but will that change? Will it revert to how it was?

I inhale deep and release the breath slowly, attempting to organize my thoughts. What happened shouldn't matter because it won't erase who I am to Maximus or his apparent hatred for my father. However, I can't say I'll leave this bed unaffected. If anything, I can almost guarantee that leaving unscathed is as unlikely as Maximus falling in love with me.

Would I even want that?

I want love, but Maximus doesn't know how to give it. And the truth is I may not know how to receive it even if he did.

Shoving that notion aside, I go back to my original musings. What will happen now? My heart flutters in my chest at the idea of him treating me the way he did last night. And my heart threatens to crack at the notion of him going back to wanting to hurt me.

That shouldn't matter.

He shouldn't matter.

But…he does.

Maximus is due to leave the country tomorrow, so I only have to make it through twenty-four hours, and then I'll have the time to properly analyze the things that are happening to me as well as the emotions bombarding me. I won't miss him, but I'm nervous to be without his protection. If he hates me, his brothers most likely do too. Will they finish what Maximus has started concerning me?

My body trembles at the images of me being at the mercy of those two strangers or Maximus's men. I've had to admit to myself that my husband's touches haven't been traumatic because of my idealistic view of him, originating from my interaction with him as a young girl. He was so noble to want me protected, but there was more to it than that. Maximus didn't agree with the ideals held by the other men in the underworld, and for a girl constantly berated by her father for my unruly behavior, Maximus was a beacon of hope. He represented the husband I wanted, and even at an early age, I recognized him for the unique man he was.

He was... That's the source of my grief when it comes to him.

"Emilia?"

The rumble of his voice stills me; even the shaking coursing through me a second ago comes to a halt. That is the power of the command he has over me, to prompt my body to obey at the mere sound of his voice. Adding that authority to his usage of my name? I'm all but paralyzed in shock. He has never once addressed me as such. A part of me flares with a strange hope, one too fragile to take flight, and I quickly suffocate it with reality.

Maximus calling me by my name means nothing.

I turn my head in his direction in lieu of giving an answer and then remember his edict for me to always acknowledge him. "Yes, sir?"

He blinks in rapid succession, and I wonder if it's from the morning light or from his confusion at my response. Did he want me to call him by name as well? Did I miss the opportunity to do so? Not that it matters, since the moment has passed.

"Have you been awake long?" he asks. His tone is lazy and gruff from sleep, and I have to battle the way it threatens to endear him to me.

I shake my head. He stares at me, in that studious way of his, and the light shining brightly through the floor-length windows strips away all feelings of security. It's as if he can see everything, perhaps more now than ever before. Sex with him has made me more vulnerable, more exposed than I've ever felt in my life. I know a woman's brain releases a chemical during breastfeeding and sex that assists with her connecting with the other person, but that doesn't make it any easier to deal with these emotional tethers wrapping around my husband. What's worse is he doesn't experience them, leaving me to deal with this tenderness, this weakness, alone.

It doesn't take long for me to avert my gaze, unable to handle the way his pierces mine. Maximus has never approved of me looking away even though he says he enjoys submission. I don't get the inconsistency of his words and actions, but then again, I don't understand many things about people, especially him.

He lightly grips my breast and thumbs my nipple, causing me to squeeze my thighs together. "Did you get enough rest?" When I nod enthusiastically, the corner of his mouth tilts upward just a little. I interpret that half smile to mean he's aware I'm answering him quickly so he'll remove his hand.

Which I simultaneously do and don't enjoy only because I'm conflicted emotionally about everything.

"Are you sure?" he asks, his tone sly. I give him another vigorous nod, and it pulls up both his lips. "Look at me."

I fortify myself before I do, unsure of what I'll find. It's much safer to view him from my peripheral vision. He grins at me, and the pressure in my chest sends alarm streaking through me. It was just sex, nothing more. But that logic doesn't erase the way he's looking at me, without hatred and malice. I wouldn't go so far as to say there's a light emotion there, but just having the dark ones gone is a reprieve I needed but didn't hope for.

His hand drifts from my breast down to glide over my rib cage and then settle on my hip. The heat from his palm scorches me, and his fingers brand me with the way they cling to my skin in a possessive manner. "You're coming with me to France. With that being said, Rosetta will have her hands full getting you a wardrobe in less than twelve hours, so be prepared for her to be surly."

Is there a word in the English language that goes beyond *speechless*?

Questions cycle around and around in my mind, gaining momentum with every pass. Why am I going with him? When did this decision happen? What will I do there? The confusion is blatant on my face, and I don't try to hide it. This doesn't make any sense at all.

He squints at me, and creases appear at the corners of his eyes. "Do you have a problem with this?" His hold on the curve of my hip tightens. Whether it's in thought or in warning, I'm not able to discern. "Answer me."

I open my mouth to speak, and nothing comes. My heart pounds at the look of barely concealed anger on his face, and I swallow the nerves threatening to choke me. Maximus follows the movement, his eyes focused on my neck as if he's considering strangling me.

"I don't have a problem, sir."

Once again I drop my gaze. And once again he orders me to bring it back to him with the simple clearing of his throat. "Don't lie to me," he says, his tone like a razor, sharp and cutting. "You acted like I ordered you to fucking stab yourself. Tell me why. Now."

"I..."

"Emilia."

My words flow from me in a rush, leaving me no time to enjoy the thrill derived from him using my name. Again. "I don't understand why. I assumed you'd want to be rid of me, and a business trip is the way to do it. Having a wardrobe is just as surprising as the trip, since it serves no purpose either." I pull as much oxygen into my body as I possibly can and take a chance on saying something I shouldn't. "So why are you doing this, Maximus?"

I watch his face, eager to discover if me using his name affects him as much as it does me when he says mine. His brows draw together, and his mouth thins, and that's the only response. I can't interpret that, but if I had to guess, I'd gather he's not pleased by what I've done.

This means I won't do it again.

"You don't need to know why," he says, retracting his hand from me. The rejection stings, although it's not unexpected. I gambled and lost. "And you don't have an opinion on the subject either, *donnaccia*. I can't have my wife"—he sneers the word—"fucking naked in Paris, even if she is a whore. And I don't need my brothers or my men trying to fuck you behind my back. Be grateful I allow you to have clothing."

The pain spreading through me is as though Maximus just crushed my chest with the heel of his boot.

I've been waiting for this man to surface. Whatever person lay with me in the bed a moment ago is gone. I'm not certain whether I'm the cause of Maximus's anger or if the tenderness from earlier was an illusion to begin with, a mirage created by my mind because of the hunger I have for human connection.

But I want it with the man in front of me.

"Thank you, sir." My voice is small and meek. And I hate it.

He is back to his normal self, and so am I. Both of us are playing the roles assigned to us by him and maybe even by circumstances of the past. All in all, they dictate our future, or my future with him at the very least.

And it doesn't look promising.

I STARE up at the metal stairwell leading into the private jet, and once Maximus reaches the platform at the top, he turns around.

"Come here, *donnaccia*."

"Yes, sir."

My voice is still small and demure, which is how it's been since yesterday morning when Maximus informed me I was to accompany him to France. Whatever changes I thought may have occurred are nothing more than a distant memory.

I grip the railing and concentrate on putting my high-heel-covered foot on the next stair, because if I don't, I'll tumble to the ground in a disgraceful heap. Once my step is secure, I repeat the process. I haven't worn shoes in years, not having a need for them in the sanctuary of my room, and they are as foreign to me as the sun shining overhead. The warmth from it covers me, and I inwardly smile, but it quickly fades at the vexation on Maximus's face. Regardless, I breathe in the fresh air and soak up the sun while I can. Who knows how long it'll be until I experience the outdoors again after this trip?

When I get to the top of the stairs, Maximus pivots and enters the aircraft, leaving me to follow. I take in the opulent surroundings, noting the tans, beiges, and other warm colors that cover the furniture and the walls. Otello, Dante, and Leone are already there, along with a female flight attendant.

All of it is forgotten with the roaring of the engines.

I jump when someone lays a hand on my shoulder. My chest spasms, and I whip my head around to find Maximus gazing down at me with his brows gathered in irritation.

He indicates one of the elaborate chairs that's basically a recliner. "Go sit and strap yourself in."

"Yes, sir."

His men's gazes shoot to me, and I walk over to the designated seat on wobbly legs. When I lower myself onto the nicely cushioned chair, Maximus's expression has soured to the point where he looks at me like he wants to throttle me. I busy myself with the seat belt, confused as to why he's upset with me. However, there's nothing to be done about it. He thinks what he wants, and I've given up trying to understand his convoluted logic.

The captain's voice sounds and carries through the sound system, notifying everyone present of the upcoming takeoff. Even before the plane has begun taxiing down the runway, I'm closing my eyes and offering prayers of supplication.

I've never flown before.

Although I know it's safer than driving, the noises and shaking from the plane grate on my frazzled nerves, which only heightens my anxiety. I'd give anything to swallow one of those pills my father used to give me, because they put me into a stupor and blurred reality to the point I couldn't be concerned with much of anything.

"Donnaccia."

"Yes, sir?" I ask, squeezing my eyes shut at hearing his voice. He's so close he must be in the seat next to me. The click of the seat belt confirms my guess.

"Look at me."

I shake my head, frantic at the idea of seeing the plane leave the ground. Or plummet. I've never openly defied Maximus. Doing this in front of his men is enough to garner severe punishment, but I can't help it. I'm more frightened of crashing to my death than my malicious husband.

"You," Maximus snaps. I flinch at his tone and wait for him to grab me and force my compliance. "Get me a drink. Alcohol."

There's a feminine sound of someone clearing their throat. "Sir, we are in the middle of takeoff. It's not safe. I'd be happy to—"

"You'd be happy to do what the fuck I'm telling you to. Get me a drink and do it right the fuck now." Maximus grinds his molars, and I'm surprised I can make out the sound despite the noise all around me. *"Donnaccia."*

I disregard Maximus as the plane's front wheels lift from the ground and the pressure from takeoff smashes me into the cushions. A small whimper tumbles from me, and for once I don't care about the show of weakness. There's nothing that can get me to ignore my instincts, which are screaming for me to protect myself from the invisible forces of gravity.

"Emilia." His voice is gentler than before, but even the sound of my name on his tongue can't pull me from the cloud of terror surrounding me.

Vaguely I make out the footsteps heading in my direction. "Here you are, sir."

Maximus shifts next to me and then says, "Emilia, look at me."

I attempt to take in enough oxygen to answer him, but all it does is make my breathing jagged and thin. I'm hyperventilating. I know this, and I can't stop it. My nails dig into the supple armrests, and my fingers cramp from the death grip I employ. A low moan tumbles from me when the plane dips, and my stomach rises to my throat.

"Fuck." There's the sound of Maximus releasing his seat belt, and then he's doing the same to me. "Come here, Emilia."

A mewl of protest is all I can manage. I know him undoing the safety belt won't matter, but it serves to push me over the edge mentally. "Maximus, please. Please don't. Don't do this."

He mutters under his breath right before he moves and grabs my hips, plucking me from my chair. I gasp, and by the time

I'm ready to fight him, he's placing me in his lap. He positions me sideways, his clean-shaven jaw touching my forehead and his muscled torso pressing against my hip and arm.

"You're safe," he whispers in my hair, his breath stirring the tendrils that came loose at the frenzied shaking of my head earlier. I'm still too scared to fully believe him, but I mentally cling to those words.

Then I'm clinging to him with a small shriek as the plane dips once more.

I snake my arms around his neck and bury my face in the warm space where his shoulder meets his throat, while tucking my legs so they're close to my chest. There's no logic to be found in my actions. Only my instincts, which drive me to Maximus.

He is strength personified, and if anyone can protect me, it's him.

"Tell me the statistics of traveling on a plane," he says. He wraps his arms around me, and my heart sighs. "You can compare it to that of any transportation, if you wish."

Facts bombard my panic-riddled brain, and before I've had a chance to really think, they practically fall from my lips. I have yet to open my eyes, but I find keeping them closed helps tremendously. However, not as much as my husband holding me.

"Fact: More than 80 percent of the world's population is afraid of flying. And only 5 percent has ever been on a plane."

"Good girl," he murmurs. "That's very interesting. Anything else you want to add?" When I shake my head, he cups my face. His palm takes up the entirety of my cheek, as well as my jaw, once again emphasizing and reaffirming how much bigger and stronger he is than me. He traces my bottom lip with his thumb, coating it with liquid, the touch light and nonintrusive. "Taste that."

The burning scent of the alcohol hits my nose, and I wrinkle it slightly before I flick out my tongue. Maximus swallows deep, his throat working against my forehead. A flare hits my taste buds. "Again," he says, his voice now gruff. I obey, and after that the rim of a glass taps my mouth. "Drink this and don't stop."

He doesn't give me time to rebel or comply. The liquid gathers at my mouth, and I have no choice but to part my lips or else the contents will spill onto us. I gulp down the liquor, ignoring the burning trail it creates going down. It settles in my belly, and the warmth collets there, heating me from the inside.

But it's his praise that lights a fire in me.

"Good girl." He removes my high heels and tosses them to the floor. It's strange to have his hands on my feet, gripping my ankle in an almost tender way, and then him wrapping his arms around me once more. Against my better judgment, I snuggle into his massive frame, into him. "The alcohol should make you more comfortable, little one."

All my terror from before is slowly morphing into something else. Something alluring like desire. My body all but melts into Maximus, and I sigh before I can stop myself. This moment in his embrace is everything to me. He may hate me, be my enemy, and hurt me, but I've never felt more cherished by a man. It's fucked up and wonderful and insane.

And I don't care.

He takes my chin between his fingers and nudges it up, causing me to shake my head in an attempt to dislodge his hold. I want to stay in this place of safety and comfort for as long as I can.

I may never experience it again.

"You can't hide from the world," he says quietly. "There are many bad things you won't see coming, but you'll also miss the things that are good. Open your eyes." Just as I'm about to refuse, he turns his head and his lips brush my temple. The shivers racing through me are purely sexual. There is no fear to fall back on, to use as an excuse. "I promise you won't regret it," he says.

Perhaps it's the seductive tone of his voice, which could get me to do just about anything right now. Or maybe it's my curiosity. Either way, I nod and slowly lift my eyelids. He nudges my chin and stares down at me. There's a shift, a softening in his gaze as he looks at me. My body recognizes it before my mind does, and my pulse turns rapid.

He breaks the connection by gesturing to the window. "Go see."

I'm not secure enough on my own to brave facing my fear, so I adjust myself in his lap and then tentatively peek out the window. The clouds are so close I'm able to make out the texture of them, which looks like cotton.

"Fact: The National Transportation Safety Board gathers aviation data concerning accidents," I say. "They say there is a one in 7,178 chance of death from flying."

His lips skim my cheek. "What else?"

I can't discern if he's asking me because he wants to know or not, but I tell him anyway. Data has been a constant companion for me, and I have a fierce need to share it with Maximus. I don't dwell on the reason for that, since it's not something I want to acknowledge.

"Fact: Statistically speaking, flying is safer than driving." I stop for a moment and drink in the breathtaking scenery thousands of feet below us. My fear has all but disappeared, and my love for experiencing new things swells. "And it's beautiful." I smile up at him and absently draw circles on his nape, just under his hairline. "Thank you for helping me see that before it's too late."

His eyes gleam, and I stiffen.

There's no time to protect myself. My arms are still wrapped around his neck, leaving me open for anything, and it's not as if I could truly escape anyway. Being on this plane ensures I'm more of a captive than ever before. When his cock hardens against my hip, I suck in a breath. Maximus's gaze lands on my mouth, his intent clear.

Then his lips are on mine.

I freeze at this. He's never kissed me before. And it's my first, leaving me confused as to what I'm supposed to do. Not to mention his men are probably watching. It's one thing to sit on his lap in front of them, but it's another to be intimate.

The sensation of Maximus's tongue plunging between my lips has me shutting out the world, eager to enjoy this new discovery. He gets to his feet with me in his arms and heads to the rear of the plane, but my eyes are closed by then because all I can think about is the way he's swirling his tongue, flicking it, and running it along the outline of my mouth.

After closing the bedroom door with his foot, he lays me down on the bed. Then I lock my arms around his neck, yanking him to me. His small huff of laughter brushes my lips as he positions his body over mine. Then he's devouring me. Exhilaration soars within me at the intensity of his hunger. And it's building with every stroke and every caress.

Can kissing be just as intimate as sex? In this moment, for this woman, it is.

Maximus pulls his mouth from mine, and I make a sound of protest, which has him grinning at me. My heart flips in my chest at the beauty of it, but then my heart nearly stops at his words.

"I'm going to fuck you, Emilia. Right here and right now," he says, his eyes glittering with something beyond lust. "I'm telling you, not asking, so offer your cunt to me or I'll be forced to take what I need."

"Do it."

His gaze widens, his pupils contracting before his eyes search my face intensely. I nod once to affirm what he's not asking, and Maximus's expression turns savage. Within seconds, our clothes are discarded on the floor, long forgotten. He runs his hands the length of my body before grabbing the backs of my thighs in a tight grip. My husband doesn't waste any time and thrusts into my body with a tortured groan.

"You're always ready for me." He says this with a tone laced in ecstasy and disbelief. "So fucking wet and still tight even though I've pounded the fuck out of you."

I can only respond with a moan and digging my nails into his back, needing him closer. I want him in me, on me, with me. I want his air in my lungs, and his touch imprinted on my skin. I want his words in my mouth and his kisses on my lips. This need must be what he mentioned before, a consuming, primal desire to obtain relief, but it's more than that.

It's the connection between two people, a union of not only bodies but souls.

My husband rides me long and hard until I'm shaking with the need to come, followed by the need to scream. My orgasm hits me at my core, and I spiral into an abyss where pleasure envelops me, as does Maximus's arms. He laces our fingers, holding on to me but letting go of his control. His groan of release is muffled against the skin of my neck, and his breaths take a long while to slow.

In the time it takes my heart rate to normalize, I lie there in a state of euphoria and confusion. Maximus kissed me. Why? To soothe my fears or distract me? I doubt the latter was his motivation because I was nearly calm by that time. Asking him wouldn't be worth the humiliation, and I don't want him to gain an inkling of what it meant to me.

He lifts his head, and I hide my thoughts with a neutral expression. "Are you all right?" he asks. I nod with a blush heating my cheeks at the informality of the question. Maximus scans my face and cocks his head, causing his hair to sway. My fingers twitch with the desire to touch him openly and without reprimand.

"Was that your first kiss?" He makes a clicking sound with his tongue when I turn my head and brings my gaze back to his by taking my chin in hand. "You always hide your eyes when you don't want to answer, but you'll find I'm relentless in getting what I want."

I know that about him, on a deeper level than he might think.

"Yes," I whisper. Heat floods my cheeks as soon as the admission leaves me. The embarrassment within me compounds at the widening of his eyes. "Why do you always ask me such personal questions?"

Immediately I clamp my lips together, scolding myself for talking back to him. I have no idea how he'll react, and it's not like I've been able to understand or foresee his actions lately. Maximus hasn't been behaving how he did the night we got married, so every word, every look, is similar to a game of Russian roulette. I could win, or I could lose.

Badly.

"I—"

He places his finger to my lips, smothering the apology forming there. I search his gaze for a hint of emotion, whether negative or not. As usual, his expression is indiscernible.

"I ask you," he says, dropping his hand from my mouth, "because I want confirmation."

"I don't understand. If you already suspected, then why does my say-so matter?"

"I want—no, *need*—to hear you say it." Maximus tucks a strand of my hair behind my ear, and my insides warm. "I can't explain it."

"There are plenty of other women who are without experience. Maybe not because their fathers kept them prisoner for years, but still."

Maximus's eyes narrow infinitesimally at the mention of Caruso, and I hope I haven't ruined this moment by bringing up my father. He's relevant to the conversation but not to my life.

"There are women who are pure," Maximus says, bringing my attention back to him. "However, they are not pure of heart."

I shrug. "No one is."

He gives me a strange look. "I believe you are."

"No." I shake my head several times, and he arches a brow. "I'd happily shoot my father." I sigh and purse my lips. "I'm glad you hate him as much as I do, because like you said earlier, you're relentless in getting what you want, so it's only a matter of time before he's dead. I will rest easier knowing my father is gone, but I do rest easy now just knowing you're going after him."

Maximus stares at me, and I blink up at him. "What is it?" I ask.

"You." He grins at me. "You are nothing like I thought you'd be."

I don't tell him he was everything I feared him to be at first but now he's beginning to remind me of the guardian angel he proclaimed to be several years ago.

I hope he can protect me once again by stopping me from giving him my heart.

MAXIMUS

I've been to France, Paris specifically, on many occasions, and its glamour has dulled for me, making it nothing but another city in which to conduct business.

But to Emilia? Paris is heaven on earth.

She fairly bursts with the excitement she's trying to keep hidden. My mouth pulls to the side in a frown. Why is Emilia attempting to dampen her enthusiasm? I know right away I'm the reason. She must fear I'll somehow use it against her, and she would have been right.

If not for the moment she smiled at me.

For the first time.

It was like a bullet to the chest. I couldn't breathe from the impact it had on me. All at once I saw her, truly and completely, and fully grasped the stunning creature in my arms was, and is, my bride.

Mine and no other's.

I've never been one to concern myself with religious practices more than attending the occasional mass and confession, but right then, I wanted to be honor bound to her until death. The Silvestri family motto now applied to Emilia. Not because she was my tool for revenge or my property.

It's because she's my wife. Mrs. Silvestri and nothing less.

That train of thought led to many things, starting with her first kiss. Now there are other firsts she wants to experience. And by watching her, I'm going through it all, viewing it in a different light. Or maybe just light in general, since my norm is a world of darkness.

When my father hid my brothers and me, after our mother's disappearance, he never left the underworld. It was where I was born and raised and where I will die. But Emilia, despite being brought up in the same environment, still shines as though reflecting the sun's light.

Or maybe she *is* the sun.

Her small gasp of surprise has me gripping my weapon and swinging my gaze from side to side in the hotel room, my entire body tense from anticipating danger until I find the source of her disquiet. She's pressed against the balcony door like a child trying to gain a vantage point at an aquarium. And beyond her is the Eiffel Tower in the distance, the dark of night lit by the structure covered in thousands of light bulbs.

Their glow pales in comparison to the joy on her face.

"What are you looking at?" I ask, letting my hand fall away from my weapon.

Her spine goes erect, and I clench my teeth at her reaction to me. I prefer her soft and pliant or wet and panting for me, not scared and skittish. Although I can't blame her, my irritation is there nonetheless.

She drops her gaze, a telltale sign she doesn't wish to share her thoughts. "The city, sir."

"What about it?" I walk over to her, watching how her eyes widen at my approach. When I'm by her side, the shine that made the green all but sparkle is nearly gone. Was it always there and I've missed it this entire time? And if not, what has caused it to return?

Emilia twists her fingers in the fabric of her clothing. "It's beautiful."

"Do you wish to see it?"

I'm just as stunned at my invitation as she is. What in the fuck am I thinking? We are not tourists, and the only reason we have a day before the meeting with Charles Fontaine is because I never do business while jet-lagged. I can't have my judgment impaired in any way when making decisions, most importantly the ones that could cause me or my brothers to end up dead.

Apparently my judgment is impaired when it comes to my wife.

"Is...is that okay?" She bites her bottom lip, another tell of hers. Upon seeing that, I have half a mind to say no so I can fuck her until we both can't walk. Emilia does that shit with her lip all the time, and I like it as much as it drives me insane. "It's late at night...," she says, letting her voice disappear.

I wave a hand in dismissal. "It's fine."

She glances at the glass door, looking beyond to the city with a longing so potent I can almost touch it. When she brings her gaze to mine, there's a vulnerability there. It's fragile and must be handled with care or I may not ever witness it again. "Are you sure?"

I nod, and the effect is immediate. Her smile returns, and I want to kiss her, to taste what pure innocence of the soul is like. Would mine taint hers?

Or could hers possibly cleanse mine?

"Yes," I rasp, my voice thick with the need overtaking me. And it's more than sexual.

"Thank you! I'll just grab my—"

I grip Emilia's upper arm and swing her to me. Her chest collides with mine, curves molding to muscle. Everything about her is welcoming. From her parted lips, which can graze my tongue, to the wet heat between her legs, which can envelop my cock, her body is a haven.

My mouth is on hers, claiming every inch of it. Her lips are soft and warm, and she fuses herself to me without hesitation. Her yielding to me is not a sign of weakness. I thought so when I first met her, but no longer. Emilia gives in because she knows she'll be the one left standing through any type of confrontation. Her will is strong, formidable enough to withstand everything she has and still allow her to smile. My joy died before it had a chance, yet when I'm around my wife, I'm able to feed off hers.

And that is more than I ever thought to have.

She moans, a fucking sexy little sound that has my cock harder than before I took her mouth. Even though I want to run my hands all over her, I don't because once I start, I won't be able to stop. Emilia has never asked for anything, either good or bad. I've given her misery, but now I want to give her a bit of happiness.

However much my selfishness will allow.

I pull back to look down at her flushed face and swollen lips. She breathes heavily, pressing her breasts into me, and I bite back a groan. I really shouldn't have kissed her. However, now I know what joy tastes like.

It's found in her, and it shows through her smiles.

And like the fucking asshole I am, I don't want anyone else to have them.

"Grab your coat," I say.

It takes a second for the glazed look to leave her eyes, but the shine quickly returns. She throws on her coat and scarf, and then smiles. That one, like all the others, fucking belongs to me.

I hold out my hand, and she takes it, albeit tentatively. Then a short while later, we are walking outside in the cool night air. Dante, Otello, and Leone follow at a distance, and I doubt Emilia knows of their presence. Even if she does, I bet she doesn't care.

She is too busy living.

Her emerald eyes land on everything, and when I catch her studying something for longer than a handful of seconds, I ask her about it. She's animated and bubbly when I do. Emilia tells me everything she's ever learned about the history of the place or any hidden meanings pertaining to it. Her enthusiasm is infectious, and I can't take my gaze from her.

"I think you know more than the internet," I say.

Her brows draw together, causing her forehead to crease. She obviously doesn't realize I'm joking with her, and I have the strongest urge to smooth out her worry lines.

"I'm teasing you, little one."

Her full lips form a perfect circle. "I thought I was boring you." When I shake my head, her entire face relaxes. "I'm glad."

"What about this?" I ask, pointing to a well-known statue. I've seen it on numerous occasions, but hearing the details come from Emilia makes it as though the figure is about to come to life. "At the rate we're going, we'll never make it to the Eiffel Tower before dawn." I wink at her to ensure she knows I'm not being serious, and a pretty blush settles on her cheeks.

"Dawn?" She scoffs. "It'd be faster to have Father Aldo go through your list of sins than to have me sightsee." She glances at me tentatively, but then the green of her eyes sparkles with mischief. "And that would take *quite* a while."

A laugh escapes me, surprising us both. She giggles in response to that. And now I've found another thing I wish to taste. Can I make her laugh again? I've never tried to amuse a woman, and the thought gives me pause. This is because I've never cared enough to even consider it let alone try.

"I've lost track of the time," she says, glancing around as though she's been pulled from a dream and thrust back into reality. In a way, I guess she hasn't experienced it much, since Caruso kept her under lock and key. I have no regrets that Emilia was innocent and has only known my touch, but her fucking cocksucker of a father did her no favors. He took the world from her.

And I will make it hers to rule over.

My initial instincts were correct: she is a queen.

"We can go now, sir." Her voice is filled with intense longing and disappointment. "I know you have...things to attend to. And we've been out for a long time..."

Again, she averts her gaze. And again, I bring it back to me, anchoring her to me by sliding my arm around her waist. She places her hands on my chest, and I'm not sure whether she thinks to push me away or not. Then a spark of heat flares in her eyes, and the emerald within looks like burning embers, the color turning to peridot. I'll never get tired of seeing her like this, as though she's eager for me to take her.

I nod, and she reluctantly does the same, her internal flame dimming. "You're right," I say. "I have many important things to do, but *this* is one of them."

"Maximus," she breathes. At the way she says my name with adoration, my cock twitches, then hardens. I've never allowed her the use of my name at her leisure, yet on the rare occasions I have heard it, she was experiencing intense emotion. It's almost as if she forgets herself and goes to what feels natural, which I find astounding. Does she see me for the man I am, not only the monster?

If so, I want her to continue doing that.

I raise my hand to grip the back of her neck in a hold that more than shows my possessive thoughts concerning her. She parts her lips on an inhale, and I refrain from taking her mouth. Again.

"You said my name," I tell her. Emotions skate across her face, and most are gone before I can label them, but fear is the one I do latch onto. "Why?"

"I forgot. I'm sorry, sir."

"You needn't be." She squints up at me, and I offer reassurance by running my thumb along the side of her neck in soothing strokes. "If I may call you Emilia, then you may use my given name. It is only fair."

That glorious smile returns, the one that makes me want to fuck her until I die.

"Very well, Maximus."

I groan. "Let's continue on before I get us both arrested by stripping you naked and fucking your tempting body. And mouth."

She presses her lips together, and a tantalizing glint appears in her gaze. "Fact: According to article 222-32, 'Publicly visible sexual exhibition in public zones are punishable by one year of imprisonment and 15,000 euros.' However, I think you can afford it."

A bark of laughter bursts from me. "You are trouble."

I finally release her and reclaim her hand. The night continues on with her telling me about all the things she's learned and with my cock hard as fuck the entire time.

It's possibly the best night of my life.

By the time we reach the Eiffel Tower, Emilia is speechless. I find that I miss her incessant talking and the sound of her voice, but the wonder in her gaze more than makes up for it. She thanks me for taking her here, and the way she says it has me wanting to give her anything, if she would continue to speak to me like that.

I shove that thought aside as quickly as it arises. There's a difference between allowing her to explore France and giving her anything. Some things aren't fucking accessible to anyone.

Not even the one woman I'd consider giving my soul to, in order to see her smile.

~

THE WAY my wife's cunt squeezes my cock is something I may never get used to.

And I don't want to.

Her soft cries fill my ears as I fill her, pushing as deep as I can so that every part of me is surrounded by her. My orgasm hits me like a punch to the gut, and my body convulses before I come, marking what is mine.

And Emilia is *mine*.

That is a truth I can no longer ignore.

I drop my head in the curve of her shoulder and inhale the scent of her. Violence has always brought out the primal side of me, but Emilia triggers it like nothing else. That is why I run my nose along her neck and then bury it in her hair to inhale deep. She wears a light perfume, and only because Rosetta packed it, but it serves to enhance her natural scent. Which I can't get enough of.

She sighs wearily, and I grin. Emilia might be exhausted now, but it was she who threw down the gauntlet earlier. If last night in the city was the best in my life, then waking up to her sucking my cock is the best morning of my life. Just thinking about that has it stiffening.

"Again?" she whispers, astonishment coating her tone.

"Is that a problem?"

"No."

"But?" I prompt. I don't like the note of worry in her voice. The need to see her facial expression has me lifting my head. "What is it?"

She blinks up at me and adjusts under me. If it's a hint for me to remove myself from her, she's got another fucking thing coming. Being inside her is the only thing that brings me peace. I don't understand it, and I don't have to.

But I can't deny it either.

"It's nothing really," she says. Her smile is bright, but it's too much, reminding me of a fake gem instead of a real one. She's not exactly lying to me, yet she damn well isn't telling me the whole truth.

"Nothing, hmm?" I palm her breast, and she presses into my hold. This is the way she is with me; I touch her, and Emilia gravitates to me. If I wanted to get pissed the fuck off, I'd consider she's this way because I'm the only male to awaken her sexually, but I don't. "Then why'd you question me?"

"I'm sorry, sir."

That has me grinding my molars. The only things I want on her tongue are my name, my cum, and my cock. She reverts back to "sir" whenever she gets nervous, and even though it's a rule I subjected her to, I hate it.

"Don't apologize. Answer the question." She bites her bottom lip, and I pinch her nipple hard so that she releases it. "Emilia…"

Her face turns bright red, and I listen for sounds of her breathing to make sure she isn't choking. It helps me relax, somewhat, when she inhales. "I'm sore." The words are said so quietly I almost don't hear them despite being less than six inches from her mouth.

As soon as their meaning registers, a heaviness settles on my chest. I attribute it to guilt, but since my focus is on her, I don't explore that. Of course her body is tired. I've only fucked her like an animal several times, thinking only of what I wanted. It's true she wanted it also, and I'm not a selfish lover, always making sure to pleasure her to the point of madness, but I didn't stop to consider how new this is to her.

I pull out of her slowly, and she winces, which has me muttering curses under my breath. Her expression is crestfallen, but it quickly turns surprised when I pull her into my arms and head toward the bathroom. She says nothing the entire time I prepare the jacuzzi-sized tub, wash her languidly from head to toe, and then towel her dry. Some of my movements are rough, seeing as this is not something I've done except once before, and not one time does Emilia complain. Actually, with every minute that passes, she blossoms under my ministrations, much like she does when I stroke her erogenous zones. I make a mental note of that and order her to get dressed.

After seeing to my own hygiene, I exit the bathroom to find her ready. I'm still fuming over my thoughtlessness concerning her, and it threatens to spill over, which I don't want. Emilia is as silent as the city's catacombs, and I aim to rectify that immediately as well as make up this oversight on my part. The one thing I won't do is dig deep into why I'm thinking this way about my bride.

"Are you hungry?" I ask. She gives me a curt nod, and it bothers me, but I understand it. I've forced her to reveal her discomfort and obviously embarrassed her. "Is there anything in particular you want?"

"The love lock bridge."

Her childlike enthusiasm from last night has returned, much to my relief. The side of my mouth tilts up. "To eat?"

"Oh!" She's quiet for a moment and then says, "Anything, as long as we eat outside."

"Consider it done."

The light returns to her eyes.

And I make sure it stays there throughout the entire day. During breakfast she talks animatedly about any- and every-thing while I listen with genuine interest. I knew she was intelligent and educated, but seeing it manifest is captivating. Not more than the way Emilia's face flushes from excitement paired with the chilly fall air.

No matter what we do, it's mundane. Yet I've never been more content. Being away from the demands of the family business, my brother's expectations, and my own for a short time is a freedom I can't quite comprehend. For so many years, since I can remember, my life has been full of nothing but revenge. Here with Emilia, I'm just a man with his wife.

I don't know if it can get better than that.

When we finally make it to the love lock bridge that looks over the Seine River, she stops and simply stares at the amassed locks, which seemingly take up every inch of the bridge's railings. Couples mill about, and I scan them thoroughly before dismissing them as a threat. I may be here as a guest of the *Brise de Mer*, but their rival gang may not take kindly to the business negotiations I have in mind.

It's always best to be vigilant rather than dead.

Emilia brings me out of my thoughts and garners my attention by clasping her hands and pressing them to her chest. She inhales deeply and closes her eyes. I wait, unsure of what's going on with her. This is similar to a religious experience or something of that nature. Then she opens her eyes, and the shine of tears reflects the sunlight.

The sight of her upset has me closing the distance between us, and right when I'm about to grab her, she turns to me.

"I want a lock, Maximus." Emilia reaches out to touch one of the hundreds within her range and then retracts her arm. "These are someone else's, so I shouldn't…"

I'm careful not to cause her alarm, but I really want to grab her and demand she tell me what she's thinking about. Instead, I dip my head toward the metal locks. "What are these for? I've never taken the time to notice."

She summons the courage to touch one, laying it on her palm. "People in love have their names engraved on the lock and then secure it on the bridge. Once that's done, they throw the key into the river. Fact: This tradition didn't start here. It originated in Hungary. However, the love is all that matters, and it's the only thing I want to feel."

Love is a four-letter word, but there are others that hold just as much weight and carry just as much emotion.

Pain.

Rage.

Hate.

These are things I'm familiar with. These are what kept my family energized when we had hitmen after us. They are the emotions that kept us alive when love tried to destroy us. Emilia may think she wants this from me, but I don't have it to give.

And even if I did, I wouldn't, because love makes you fucking weak.

My father's for my mother killed him and broke our family.

My love for my mother fuels me just as much as it cripples me.

I narrow my gaze at Emilia, pinning her with it. "What would you do if you felt love? What good is it?"

She frowns and worries her bottom lip between her teeth. "Love is...it will make you do something for someone you'd never consider otherwise."

Her green eyes search mine in an almost pleading manner. Is she trying to get me to understand something? Or is she seeing my newfound lenience as an opportunity to influence me?

"Sounds manipulative," I snap. "As I said before, what good can it be?" When she opens her mouth, I cut her off. "That was a fucking rhetorical question. Love is only used to grab some poor asshole by the balls so he'll be forced to do things. And the stupid motherfucker might not even realize it." I sweep my arm, gesturing to the thousands of locks surrounding us. "Cocksuckers, every single one of them. So if you want to feel that, go ahead, but it won't come from me."

Emilia blinks rapidly as though attempting to dry her tears and dips her chin in a subtle nod. Afterward she turns her back to me and plants both hands on the rail, gazing at the water. The sun has already begun to set, and every last ray bathes Emilia in a golden hue. She looks angelic, unreal, if not for the blank stare. It's haunted and dead.

I curse under my breath and take up a spot next to her but leave a foot between us. She doesn't move, not even to bat an eyelash, and gives no indication she acknowledges I'm standing there.

This was for the best.

Emilia needed to know not to expect anything like that from me. I've already given her more than any woman, starting with a place in my bed—the one I actually sleep in—and ending with my time. I've never bestowed more than necessary on anyone and certainly never indulged them with my time in order to do frivolous things, such as dine at a bistro or walk along the Seine. However, there is nothing superficial about her smiles.

And I want them to return.

But I'll have to wait.

"I can't give you what you want," I say, keeping my eyes forward. When she doesn't respond, I turn to face her. "Emilia?"

Only because I take a step toward her does she speak.

"I wasn't talking about your love." She says the words softly and not in an accusatory way like I expected. Then she proceeds to throw me off-kilter like she always does. "I wanted to come here because I'd seen all the pictures of the couples in love, and I thought if I stood here for a moment, I could—"

She grimaces and presses her lips together, shutting me out.

Fuck that.

"Tell me," I say, my voice near a growl.

"I thought I could feel love for the first time since my mother's..." She breathes deeply several times before continuing, and when she does, my eyes go wide. "My mother's murder. I thought if I were able to be here, right in this place, to soak up the love coming from these locks—I stupidly hoped I'd feel something. Paris is the city of love, so this was my last hope."

Emilia gives me a rueful smile that makes my chest cave in on itself. "I wanted to be one of these stupid motherfuckers who felt loved."

A knife to the stomach would've been less painful than the guilt assaulting me.

And her smile has returned, but like all things in my life, I destroyed it.

How much longer until I ruin my wife completely?

EMILIA

I didn't speak for the rest of the day.

But neither did Maximus.

My sigh hits the air, and it's a small sound, a fraction of the emotions pent up inside me. The last twenty-four hours in Paris with Maximus were turning out to be my every fantasy come to life. He was attentive whenever I talked and patient for however long that took. And sometimes it was a long while. Yet he was always interested, his gaze never clouding over with boredom, or worse, irritation.

Then I ruined it by telling him about my yearning for love.

I pick up my uneaten dinner, along with the fork, and make my way to the balcony in hopes the view of the city will calm the feelings roiling within me. After I settle onto one of the chairs outside, I lose myself in the beauty of Paris.

Only for a while. Maximus is never far from my mind, even if he's no longer here.

He left for business, and I have no idea how long he'll be gone. I thought this time alone would be welcome, especially since solitude is what I'm used to. But that's not the case anymore.

I've grown accustomed to having my husband nearby.

Do I miss him? My heart answers me before my mind can tell it not to. I do. Not in a desperate way though. I just miss his ever-present strength and assertiveness. Whenever he's with me, I don't have to worry about anyone hurting me. Maximus used to be the one who frightened me, but that's changed. I can't quite figure out when or why, and it doesn't matter because it's the truth.

After today, will it all go back to the way it was?

I shudder to think so, yet this seems to be a pattern with Maximus. He is uncaring and cruel, but those interactions are dotted with tenderness that steals my breath. As much as I enjoy those gentle moments, I'd be a fool not to be wary of him and what he might do in the future.

His reasonings concerning love and vulnerability made perfect sense to me. I never want to give someone that kind of power over me. My emotions and thoughts are my own, and they are the secret things I keep hidden. Just like the locks on the bridge, I secured my heart and locked it away for safekeeping. I don't love Maximus. Yet.

But I could.

And I want to.

I'm not sure what's worse: to love him or to *want* to love him. In the end, it doesn't matter. He said I won't get that emotion from him, and I believe it. Although, I doubt I can remain unaffected like him. With each tender gesture or soft touch,

184

my walls of resistance fracture. If he hadn't gotten angry at me on the bridge, I'd be halfway in love with him. Or maybe I already am?

Like he said, what good would love do?

A shuffling sound snags my attention, and I tilt my head to make sure there's nothing amiss. The footfalls are near silent, but not completely. I grip the fork lying on my plate and press it to the length of my thigh in order to conceal it, then turn my head.

The scream in my throat never has a chance to form.

The stranger looms over me, and his features are hard to make out with the light from the room streaming behind him. "Mrs. Silvestri."

I grip the plate as though I'm going to remove it from my lap, only to hurl it at him. He dodges the porcelain missile, and I use the distraction to get on my feet. He's faster than a cobra, his hand streaking across the space between us and grabbing my outstretched arm, clamping his meaty fingers around my wrist. I aim low, knowing my tiny weapon doesn't stand a chance against the thick material of his suit. The fork prongs sink into his hand covering mine, and he bellows in rage right before he slaps me with his free hand.

Instinct has me cradling my face, covering the pulsing flesh of my cheek. But in doing that, I've left myself open for attack. The man is on me in an instant, and my cry for help is bested by darkness pulling me under.

THE SWARMING of bees brings me back into a semiconscious state.

I wince at the pounding of my head, and the minute action only exacerbates the pain. Immediately I relax my face and seek out the oblivion of sleep. Or unconsciousness.

Whatever it takes to end my suffering.

But it doesn't come. The buzzing noise that brought me back to a state of lucidity slowly morphs into voices. *Male* voices I don't recognize. My heart kick-starts in my chest, and I clench my jaw to stop myself from making any sudden movements. And also to avoid any unnecessary pain.

My brain is delayed in computing the words floating in the atmosphere around me, but eventually I understand what the people are saying.

And it's all in French.

I guess I'll see how well my self-taught language skills are.

"She's been unconscious for a long time." This voice is nasally and thin. "The boss said not to kill her, but what if she doesn't wake up?"

A gruff laugh, then a voice that's deep and similar to the male who attacked me. "She will. She's breathing, and that's all that matters."

"I don't know, what—"

"Just play your fucking hand and either ante or shut the fuck up."

The shuffling of cards is discernible and denotes their continued gameplay. While they are busy, I risk lifting my lids less than an inch. Without raising my head, I'm not able to take in much, but the zip ties binding my arms behind me and the ones on my ankles are definitely noticeable. They bite into my skin, and I guess it to be from being hunched over for however long it's been since I was taken from the hotel. There's no sunlight to detect because I'm in an office of sorts, so that's a moot point.

"You're such a fucking pussy. Call it already."

I flick my gaze in the man's direction, taking in his burly appearance. It was difficult to make out his face in the shadows when I first saw him, and the light in the room is dim, but it's enough. He's all muscle, his arms the size of my thighs, and his body is just as wide as it is tall. There's a shadow of stubble covering his square jaw, and it matches the mop of black hair on his spherical head.

Intense satisfaction warms my cold insides at the sight of the bandage on his hand where I stabbed him.

The other guy is the first one's opposite in every way. Tall and lanky with sandy-blonde hair that's in a ponytail at the nape of his neck. "I'm being cautious is all."

"Caution is for men without balls. Get on with it."

Keeping one ear tuned to their asinine conversation, I methodically check my body for injuries. The worst is the headache, and I'm grateful for the low lighting as well as the way it gives me the illusion of obscuration, however minuscule. My wrists are pretty bad off, and I worry about the minimal circulation in them and also in my ankles. Even if I was cut free this minute, I'm not sure I could run without falling. I flex my arms and legs just the slightest bit, and there isn't much give on the bindings.

Knowing I have to wait is torture. However, not knowing what I'm waiting for? That's almost unbearable. Who are these men, and why am I here? Did they kill Otello, since he was supposed to be guarding me? Those questions are the easy ones to think on and panic over. The harder ones, the ones that make me want to weep, are different. Will I be killed immediately or is there a chance I could make it out of here alive? What will Maximus do when he finds out I've been taken?

Does he even care?

My heart squeezes in agony. Of course he doesn't care. At least not in the way I want him to. He might be upset that his toy was stolen, but if I don't offer something beyond sex, then why would he? The fact I'm his wife could propel him to take action in order to save face with the rest of the underworld. Knowing Maximus? He probably doesn't give a shit what anyone thinks of him or my status as his wife.

The idea of my husband not coming for me has my soul leaving me in a rush, like a winter wind bringing with it the chill of emptiness.

But given the opportunity, I'll do whatever I can to escape, because even though Maximus doesn't want me, I still value myself and my life. My time with him, however brief, taught me a lot about myself I wasn't aware of. I'm strong. Not in the physical sense, but my mental capacity for resilience is incredible. No matter what misfortune has come my way, I've had the fortitude to get through it. My time in Paris revealed how knowledgeable I am and my capacity to learn, which will ensure I can support myself with the skills I possess. And lastly, I'm not completely broken, since I am able to love. I was very close with Maximus, and the fact I was able to generate those feelings for him leaves me stunned. I didn't think I had it inside me to be vulnerable to the point I was willing to consider emotional attachment.

And that's the thing about love: you can't deliberate it, suppress it, or control it.

Love is the most illogical emotion but absolutely the most meaningful.

The opening of the office door startles me. In walks a clean-shaven man wearing a dress shirt and pants. His pale-blue eyes remind me of tiny buttons, hard and flat, but when they land on me, I drop my gaze to the cell phone in his hand.

"Wake her up," he says.

I lift my head, not wanting to give any one of them a reason to touch me.

The bulky male pushes away from the chair and comes over to me, swallowing up my tiny frame with his large shadow. "What do you need her to do, boss?"

The newcomer holds out the phone and dips his chin in its direction.

"Someone wants to speak to you," the brute says to me in English, "but make it quick or I'll cut out your tongue. Do you understand?"

I nod, and he puts the cell phone on speaker, placing it near my mouth.

"Emilia?"

At the sound of Maximus's voice, I nearly break down. He wants to make sure I'm alive, so that has to mean something. "I'm here." The words come out cracked, and I clear my throat in preparation to speak again.

"Are you hurt?" he asks.

The boss cuts in before I can answer. He's not close to the phone, but his voice carries to me. "This is taking too long, Silvestri. You have one final question to gain confirmation, and then we'll return to the real business at hand."

"Very well," Maximus says. "Emilia, I need you to say something out of the ordinary and make sure it's nothing they could've forced you to say so I know it's not a generic recording and actually you."

I wrack my brain for something in desperation, and memories flood my mind until I'm drowning in them. There's nothing we've done in France that couldn't have been reported back to these people, and our time back in Chicago was filled with sex, which isn't original at all.

"Time's up, Silvestri. I can't help it your wife is incompetent."

I suck in a breath and let it loose on a scream, hoping I'm not too late. *"Ragazza solare!"*

"You have two hours," the boss says.

And the line goes dead.

HOURS PASS. Long, torturous hours that have me questioning my sanity.

Did Maximus really call? And if he did, was he able to hear my message?

Eventually I grow tired of mentally berating myself for my indecision, and my thoughts take a more treacherous route. Maximus might not remember the time I met him as a young girl, and that makes my proof of life null and void. He could've heard me and dismissed it as nothing more than the raving of a lunatic. Everyone, including Maximus, believed I was insane, and that could've been the evidence he needed to see it as fact.

Sunshine girl, *ragazza solare.*

A ghost of a smile tugs at my lips, and I suppress it. Maximus called me that, and I always wondered why. Did he say that because of the yellow dress I wore? Or was there something deeper he saw in me that I couldn't? The nickname was an endearment, and no one except my mother had ever given me one. Maybe that's the reason I cherished it all these years.

Well, that and because Maximus gave me hope. I wanted to marry him, since he wasn't like any of the criminals my father dealt with. When Maximus looked at me, I never felt the need to run to my mother for protection. The only feelings I got around him were safety and happiness.

I wish that were still the case.

"Come on," the brutish man says to the thinner one. Then he gets to his feet. "The boss says the negotiations are complete."

"The ones with Silvestri?"

At the mention of Maximus, I open my eyes. There's no need to pretend to be asleep, since it's apparent I'm about to be transported somewhere.

The larger man shrugs. "It didn't sound like he was willing to negotiate for her."

A part of me dies.

This stranger is only confirming what I already know, but it doesn't make the excruciating pain lessen. If my hands were free, I'd press them to my chest to stop the invisible bleeding of my heart.

"So the other one, then?"

"Yeah, he paid the ransom without complaint. Now it's time to deliver her to him."

Panic seizes me as a slew of questions fill my mind, and terror grips my insides.

If Maximus isn't coming for me, then who is?

MAXIMUS

*S*everal hours earlier...

I*T TAKES* the entire drive to the meetup location for me to get Emilia's haunted expression out of my head.

I'm right in what I said, and the resignation, as well as acceptance, was in her gaze. She knows it as much as I did that I can never love her the way she wants.

The way she deserves.

I've done a lot of fucked-up things in my life, and guilt never surfaced, because my actions were always justified. My brothers and I never hurt the innocent and never sought out retribution from those who didn't deserve it. But Emilia? I broke every code of honor I had with her for the sake of my revenge. And what happened on the love lock bridge could've been the pinnacle of my mistreatment of her. So I did what any other asshole husband would do.

I promised myself I'd make it up to her.

Although I'm not exactly sure how, I have an idea that could mend some of the hurt I've caused. Not all, but I don't know if that's even possible.

My men, Dante and Leone, flank me as we arrive at the edge of the Seine River. The area is deserted except for a couple of pedestrians making their way to warmth and shelter. It's cold, and the way the wind hits the water makes it all the more chilling. However, it's public and therefore relatively safe. I'd rather be cold temporarily than forever in death.

I heard Charles Fontaine had a flair for the dramatic, and this meeting doesn't do much to persuade me otherwise. Not with the way he walks up to me, arms open wide as if we are family.

"Silvestri, welcome."

"Fontaine," I say with a nod. "Thank you for meeting me."

The Frenchman waves a hand. "Of course, *mon ami*. How do you like my city? She is glorious, no?"

"Stunning."

He strokes his goatee with his thumb and index finger only. "I can't imagine anyone believing you're something other than a capo."

I smirk at him, keeping my gaze veiled. "Haven't you heard? I'm a wine merchant here with plans to view some vineyards and possibly purchase them. I heard they are the most profitable and contain the best soil."

"Ha! You would put a man in that expensive dirt before you'd grow grapes, that is for certain. Your reputation precedes you." He spreads his arms wide and looks heavenward. "My

194

country may not be anything close to the vastness graced to the US, but we have culture. And that, my American friend, is something you know nothing about."

I tilt my head and lift a brow. "Touché."

He wags a finger at me and grins. "Cheeky bastard. I like you. Let's discuss the terms you're looking for, and quickly so that we may drink. It is more fun anyway."

The negotiations are long and comprehensive.

Fontaine may act like a peacock, but underneath his pomp and circumstance, he's truly a vulture. There's no doubt in my mind he'd peck at my remains and clean his teeth with a shard of my bone if I didn't hold my ground and offer opposition. I've underestimated an adversary before, and I'm not about to repeat that error in judgment. He puts on a good show, and it offers a false sense of security.

Then it's my turn to impart deception when he mentions Emilia's father.

Fontaine shifts his stance, eyeing me closely. "You know Caruso's my supplier, yes? He brings me an amazing assortment of girls, and they are sold before they even arrive on my shores, hence the need for more protection. This is why I want your weapons." He thrums his fingers on the railing, the light from a nearby lamppost catching the smooth surface of the ring he wears. It's a signet one, much like the one in my family. It's passed on to the firstborn of each generation, but we lost the right to wear it when my father changed our identities. I was so young I don't even remember it or our old names.

Tristano does, and he wears the ring despite the risk it carries.

I dip my head in acknowledgment, training my focus on the dangerous man before me. "Yes, I do. But you already knew that, as well as the fact I married Caruso's daughter not too long ago."

Fontaine's lips twitch. "I was insulted when I wasn't invited to the wedding. I love a reason to celebrate and drink. Or just drink." He laughs, and the creases around his eyes deepen, but he still watches me carefully.

When I grin, it's with a slight edge to it. "The wedding happened quickly because we didn't want it to be a huge ordeal. Caruso and I were able to come to terms, and that's the long and short of it."

"Well, I hope you'll enjoy Paris and all her splendor, since this is like a honeymoon for you. We should toast to that." He snaps his fingers and spouts rapid French to one of his men, who leaves and returns with two tumblers and a decanter. After pouring two generous glasses, he hands the crystal bottle over to the bodyguard. "Here, *mon ami*," Fontaine says to me in English, his arm extended. "Let us drink to your marriage."

I lift my hand and nod in his direction. "Salute."

"Santé."

Not a drop of alcohol touches my tongue until I verify Fontaine's swallowed a portion of his. Once that happens, I take a healthy swallow of the cognac. It wards off the cool night air and burns underneath my skin, but nothing compared to the way Emilia makes me hot for her. For the umpteenth time I have to remove her from my thoughts.

However, she's brought back to my attention by fate.

Who happens to be a bitch.

Both mine and Fontaine's cell phones ring at the exact same time, and all my senses, though already on alert, go full throttle. He dips his head at me, and I do the same, pulling my mobile device from my pocket. An unknown number isn't uncommon in my line of business, but a freezing chill stabs me at the sight of it.

I answer and press the phone to my ear, then wait. If someone calls me, then they'll certainly talk, because this number is private and unable to be traced.

"Silvestri," says an unfamiliar voice. "*Bonjour* and welcome to France."

"You have me at a disadvantage, but I assume you'll rectify that by giving your identity?"

A masculine chuckle sounds, and my irritation skyrockets. "I have it on good authority you are meeting with Charles Fontaine concerning a cache of weapons. Am I correct?"

I clench my jaw to keep from cursing. This motherfucker isn't saying who he is or what he wants. I can do that as well. "Depends."

"Hmm... That's true. And what I do to your wife *depends* on you."

If time can stop, it does. If I can live without breathing, it happens.

Someone has Emilia.

The stranger's words are a poison that spreads through me, coating me with sickness and slowly killing me. With this comes the warming of my blood, and it turns my veins to tiny rivers of molten lava. This scorching heat erupts into a fury that burns with the need to exact death and vengeance.

I am going to fucking kill everyone involved. There will be no mercy, no remorse, and no hesitation on my part.

My hands shake with rage, and I squeeze the phone to halt the tremors. I shoot my gaze over to my men, and they show no outward reaction, as they've been trained. However, they both shift, bringing their hands closer to their weapons.

"How do I know you're telling the truth?" I ask, my voice flat.

"The green of her eyes is quite lovely. The tears in her eyes remind me of a pair of jewel earrings I saw once. Brilliant hue and extremely costly."

"That is not enough."

There's a pause on the other end, and then my phone beeps with a notification. I stare down at it and open the incoming message. A picture of Emilia—tied up with her eyes closed, wearing the same clothes I last saw her in—stares back at me. I'm not one to expose my thoughts, but I must be, since both my men stride to where I stand. They look at the picture and then at me, their expressions grim. I snatch up Dante's phone and quickly scroll to Gavriil's name. My enforcer takes the phone and walks away to make the call.

"Is that picture what you were wanting, Silvestri?" the voice on the phone says, taunting and smug.

I close my eyes briefly and do my damnedest to appear unaffected, keeping my tone void of the panic shooting through me. "Yes, and this is Maximus Silvestri. Now that you've confirmed my identity, it's time for me to have yours."

"I'm a member of *Unione Corse*, and we are aware of you wanting to supply someone from *Brise de Mer* with weapons. But that's going to be a problem."

"Why?" I ask.

"He is part of our rivalry. You Americans know what it's like, having someone trying to take over your territory. Fontaine will have the means to do that with your help, so call off the deal or we'll kill your wife. Slowly and after enjoying her to the fullest."

That same breathy chuckle from before scrapes my ears, and I commit it to memory, because I'm going to hear that motherfucker weep right before I slit his throat.

"What do you say, Silvestri?"

"I want proof of life and assurance she'll be kept alive and unharmed."

"Very well," the man says with a sigh. He mutters in French about tits and cunts, then raises his voice to call over someone else. "Put her on the phone. Hurry the fuck up."

There's a shuffling noise, and I'm clenching my teeth so hard to keep from losing my fucking mind that my jaw aches. Because if I hear Emilia cry out in pain, I don't know if I'll be able to stop from reacting.

"Someone wants to speak to you," a different man says in accented English. "But make it quick or I'll cut out your tongue. Do you understand?"

"Emilia?"

When I don't hear her right away, I almost crush my phone as adrenaline infused with fear rushes through my entire body. But then the sweetest sound envelops me. "I'm here."

"Are you hurt?" I ask. My voice is dark like my soul and dies a little bit with each of her panicked breaths.

The original speaker comes close enough for me to hear him. "This is taking too long, Silvestri. You have one final sentence to gain confirmation, and then we'll return to the real business at hand."

I'm going to fucking murder him.

The effort to keep from releasing the inferno of rage building within me takes every single ounce of control I possess, and my muscles protest the extraneous tension running through me.

I inhale a preparatory breath, still unsure if I'm actually speaking to her or a recording. "Emilia, I need you to say something out of the ordinary and make sure it's nothing they could've forced you to say so I know it's not a generic recording and actually you."

I'm desperate for not just the sound of her voice but the words that will let me know she's alive. And that motherfucker starts talking again.

"Time's up, Silvestri. I can't help it your wife is incompetent."

Just when I open my mouth to respond, there's a scream that slices me open, cutting me deep and leaving me in agony.

"Ragazza solare!"

The line goes dead, and my fury overtakes me until I see nothing but red, my hunger for the blood of my enemies coating my vision. Death waits.

But not for long.

MAXIMUS

I am still, quiet. Unnaturally so.

"Gavriil, this is Dante," my enforcer says into the phone. His gaze flickers to me like it has several times over the last twenty minutes. The disconcertment in his eyes mirrors that of Leone's. I must be very far gone if two of the most ruthless members of the underworld are watching me with such caution. "What did you find out?"

I'm not able to hear what's being said on the other end, but it's not hard to make out the Russian's accented baritone voice. Even his curses reach my ears. I would be amused if I weren't so focused.

Nothing matters until I find Emilia.

Dante lowers the phone and offers it to me. "He wants to talk to you."

I bring the mobile device to my ear and wait.

"Maxim," Gavriil says, using his country's version of my name, "I've told your man where we can find the girl, and

I've called all my contacts in France. Those closest to you will meet you at the location she's being held." The sound is muffled as he shouts in his native tongue, and then the distortion lifts. "My apologies, old friend. Dante told you they are en route and my allies will help you find her. Is there anything else?"

"No."

He sighs. "Ah fuck. I've never seen you this quiet. She's important, *da*?"

Gavriil has known me since the beginning of the empire my brothers and I rebuilt after losing it all. It was his connections that enabled us to create enough capital to invest in illegal arms. Now, after all these years, we are business partners as well as friends. He is one of the few people I trust. And though I don't want to discuss Emilia with anyone, I will with Gavriil because without his help I may not be able to get her back.

"My wife is...everything, Gabriel."

"She is alive, because if she weren't, that *Unione Corse* cunt wouldn't have given you time to shut down the negotiations, nor would he have texted you the address. He would've just killed her and sent you her body as a memento. This is a warning, albeit a foolish one."

Breathing becomes a challenge at the very thought of what Gavriil's saying, the vision he's creating. I *can't* lose her. Not before and certainly not after learning who she really is to me.

"This warning will be the first thing they speak to me," I say, my tether to humanity gone, "and the last will be their screams of agony after I find them."

Gavriil mutters something in Russian akin to blasphemy. "Happy hunting, Maxim. Leave none alive."

I hang up and return the phone to Dante. Then I go back to the darkest part of my mind, where Emilia's scream plays on repeat. *Ragazza solare.* The sunshine girl, who couldn't have been more than twelve years old when I met her, is all grown up and a victim of something that has nothing to do with her. I curse myself, using every foul word I can think of. That young girl was a beacon of hope for me in one of the hardest times in my life, and I always prayed she'd become a woman whose spirit was never broken and that the light in her eyes would never dull or fade. Because of me and Caruso, both have happened.

I can't decide which of us is more to blame.

When Emilia was a young girl, she asked me to marry her, since her father threatened no one would, due to her outspoken and rebellious ways. Those things I admired about her long ago are the very things I tried to destroy recently. Emilia may not be as talkative as before, but her defiance reared its head, and instead of encouraging her fiery spirit, I wanted to suffocate it.

I pray to God above Emilia still possesses that strong inner fortitude so she can survive whatever's been done to her.

If I allow my mind to go down that road, I'll be no good to her, consumed by insanity.

The entire journey to the warehouse, I clean and reload every weapon I can carry without being encumbered. With the amount of adrenaline pumping through me, I could kill everyone with my bare hands. And I still might. I've done it on several occasions, and I truly understand why serial killers choke their victims if they have an emotional connection to them. It's so fucking personal. And it's not just ending their life; it's watching their life force slowly leave their body while under your power.

It's a shame I won't be able to kill all these men.

And not more than once.

Earlier, when the phone cut off and I lost access to Emilia, I might have gone temporarily insane. There's nothing except blackness in my memory, but when I came to, I was seconds away from taking Fontaine's life. Needless to say, I may have ruined the negotiations.

I can't summon the energy to give a fuck.

"We're here," Dante says quietly. His announcement is followed by a series of weapons being cocked, mine included.

The warehouse isn't too far outside the city limits of Paris, yet every second that came after hearing Emilia's voice has been torture. I gather that feeling and use it to fuel my movements when I get out of the vehicle. Then I walk briskly to where a group of men stand off to the side of a large building with cardboard boxes littering the ground nearby.

"*Zvinite, ya ne govorju po-russki?*" I ask in Russian. The likelihood of coming across a random gathering of Russian killers isn't high, but it's not impossible either given our being in Europe. However, I'll know the second someone answers the message with a specific Italian phrase. This is something Gavriil and I have done for years to avoid trusting those not vetted by one of us.

A tall, bald man wearing cargo pants and a plain shirt under a leather vest steps toward me. "*Non parlo Italiano, mi dispiace,*" he says in Italian. Then switches to English, saying in a heavy accent, "Silvestri, I'm Vaughn. We go now."

I nod. It's all I can manage. Speaking to them about being careful not to accidentally hit Emilia in the cross fire or having them watch out for her safety won't matter if she's not here. I can't think of her being dead, not if I want to keep my focus.

And also because I don't know if I can come back from that loss.

My fucking wife is a liability, which I warned Tristano about long ago. But she's also greater than any asset I could ever possess, buy, or come across. Emilia is a gift, and I'll treat her like the queen she is or die trying.

Vaughn and his men circle around the side of the building. I trail behind them, keeping my steps light and my hand on my weapons. Dante and Leone are my silent shadows, but as grateful as I am for their loyalty, I can't concentrate on anything except getting to my wife.

The first gunshots shatter the quiet before I've had a chance to get inside, and every loud popping sound causes my gut to clench. Is that the bullet that ended Emilia's life? Or is it the one that kept her alive?

I peer around the doorframe to find an array of chaos and flying ammo. Weapons are being discharged at a rapid rate, the exchange so heavy I'm diving behind a crate nearest to me. Splinters and chunks of wood fly into the air when my barricade is hit by gunfire. I can't risk getting my head fucking blown off, but not having seen Emilia makes my blood run cold and hot all at once.

When there's a small window of coverage from my men and those with me, I lean to the side and release a barrage of bullets into the unfamiliar male close to me. I've already selected another target before his body hits the ground, and then the new mark joins his fallen comrade. In my peripheral is a streak, a flash of color, and I swing to face the bright teal, catching a glimpse of Emilia as she's dragged through a doorway.

"She's over there!" My shout is lost in the numerous sounds hitting the air all at once, but Dante and Leone, plus two of Vaughn's men, make their way in her direction. I'm closer and reach the exit first, stepping outside into the loading dock area outdoors. Only to come to a complete halt. My men, along with the Russian group, are right on my heels, and I hold out my arms wide to prevent them from taking another step.

"Stop, Silvestri, or she's fucking dead!"

I immediately raise my hands in surrender at seeing Emilia's life in danger, Caruso standing behind her with a gun pressed to her temple. My wife stares at me with a stoic expression on her beautiful face, and when my gaze connects with hers, Emilia's emerald eyes become shiny with emotion. I peruse her quickly from top to bottom, searching for major injuries, and other than Caruso threatening her, she appears unharmed. Relief threatens to swamp me, but I ignore it. There is still a very real chance my wife could end up dead.

"Isn't Paris nice this time of year?" I ask. After leaning against the exterior wall, I assume a nonchalant air and a bored expression. "I had no idea you were in town, Caruso. I don't do threesomes, so I'm not sure why you chased after me and your daughter."

"I wondered if you'd show up," he says.

"Why are you here?"

"My daughter invited me." He grins when I raise a brow in silent questioning. "Emilia's been chipped like the other trafficked girls I ship out. I've always known her whereabouts. Do you really think I'd let my opportunity for a seat within the Wolf Pack be taken from me?"

Emilia's eyes widen, allowing me to view the shock and horror within. My wife truly didn't know Caruso implanted a chip in her, and it's written all over her face.

My wife's gaze collides with mine, and she mouths, "I'm sorry," with trembling lips. The sight of her apologizing to me when she's done nothing wrong is like a heel to my windpipe. I break our connection and focus solely on that piece of shit Caruso. The very idea of him tagging her like an animal and invading her privacy is enough to make my hands shake. I cross my arms to hide signs of weakness from him. He's shrewd, and him being outnumbered and outmanned won't stop Caruso from using this situation to his advantage. It's not the first time he's exploited Emilia to get what he wanted.

But it will be the last time.

"What do you want?" I tilt my head and offer a bored expression. "I'm in the middle of a business arrangement with Fontaine, which I really need to get back to. So if you could move this the fuck along, that would be great." As I say the words, I scrutinize every man in the alley, waiting for one of them to reveal themself as the French cunt who took my wife.

Caruso grinds the barrel of the gun into Emilia's head, and she winces. His flushed face grows even redder, and I somewhat expect steam to billow from his ears. His anger doesn't compare to the wrath I'm going to invoke on him.

"It's not about what I want," he says. "I'm going to have a place in the Wolf Pack, but it can be through you or Rossi. It's up to you who ends up with her." Caruso shakes Emilia, and she doesn't make a sound. Although, the paling of her lips signals how tight his grip is on her upper arm.

I stroke my chin. "Rossi still wants her even though I've put my cock in every single part of her? Interesting..." Emilia's gaze drops to the floor. Everything I say is like acid on my tongue, slowly killing me. "I don't care if he has her, but my wife ending up with another man won't be good for business."

"Rossi is a sick bastard," Caruso says with a shrug, "and he's always been fascinated by my daughter. Fuck knows why, but it doesn't matter. The only thing I care about is the council seat, not you or the *Unione Corse*. I deliver girls to both groups, so that's your problem."

A short blonde-haired man zips his gaze to Caruso. "The Italian slut is supposed to ensure the deal with Fontaine doesn't go through." He gestures to me in sharp, jagged movements. "He'll have no reason to stop the negotiations if I don't have leverage against him, which means offering her to you was pointless," he says to Caruso.

"Pascal, you wanted to coerce Silvestri, using his wife, *and* offer my daughter to me as a means to obtain a favor," Emilia's father says. "You can't put your dick in multiple holes and expect to never catch anything."

The Frenchman's gaze narrows, and instinct has my entire body locking up with tension. Pascal's clearly not okay with how the circumstances are panning out, which means I have to watch him more carefully. He could be a powder keg, waiting for a single flame.

"I'm leaving with Emilia," Caruso says, his attention on me. "Unless you call your brother and have him nominate me to be considered in the upcoming council meeting. With his show of support, there's no reason I won't fill the vacant slot." He smirks at Pascal. "Once that's done, I don't care what happens between you and Silvestri."

A look of understanding passes between the two men, and I know my time is up.

Now I have a choice to make.

Do I sabotage my revenge against Caruso in order to save Emilia's life?

EMILIA

The steel of the gun has been pressed against my skin for so long it's no longer cold. I wonder if the bullet inside still is? I don't know much about weapons or ballistics in general, but if the trigger is pulled, I'll be dead before my brain has a chance to register pain.

I guess that's comforting.

My fear of dying is nothing compared to the agony of watching Maximus decide my fate. His face has been an expression of boredom along with the occasional mask of indifference. From his words to his body language, he doesn't care about me. At all.

It would be nice if my heart, like my brain, would die before it has a chance to register pain.

"You know that my brother's nomination isn't enough to guarantee anything," Maximus says evenly. "And I'm not going to let your greed ruin my reputation."

My father shifts his stance. "You stole her from me and from Rossi. The other families assume we made an alliance, but you and I know different. And while we're on the subject, why did you take Emilia?"

"I needed a wife to satisfy my brother's edict, and I wanted it to be someone who wouldn't play the games that women do," Maximus says. "And I don't want kids, so I don't need a woman for that." He relaxes his arms, and they fall to his sides. "I was going to have her committed when enough time had passed. The underworld believes she's fucking crazy anyway, and no one would care if I had her locked up. If you had to get married, wouldn't you want an easy out like that?"

Did I get shot? I can't feel any part of my body. Numbness coats me from head to toe and from the outside in. My heart beats, my blood flows, and my breathing continues, yet I'm dead.

Fuck all men.

My father chuckles, and even that sound doesn't anger me like it should. "You might be your brother's bitch, but I can see why he keeps you around, Silvestri. We've wasted enough time. Either make the fucking call or I'm leaving."

"Very well," Maximus says. He pulls out his cell phone, and the conversation is quick, a lot faster than I thought it'd be. Considering how much he hates my father, I thought this would be a hard decision for him.

Apparently, I was wrong. About him and so many other things.

"It's done." Maximus puts the device in his pocket and purses his lips. "You should receive an email shortly as proof my brother sent in your name to be considered."

Not more than thirty seconds later, a pinging noise sounds. My father finally removes the pistol from my skull and lowers his arm to retrieve his phone. I assume that's what he's doing, since I can't see him.

"I got it," Caruso says. "Well, she's all yours."

My father shoves me so hard I fall, landing on my hands and knees, bits of gravel tearing into my skin. Maximus takes a step toward me, but I refuse to look at him, choosing to let my hair shield me. The throbbing of my knees, which took the brunt of my impact, barely penetrates my mind.

But the gunshot does.

Already close to the ground, I flatten myself and then cover my head. All around me the loud bangs of the weapons firing cause my heart to stutter in my chest. I'm too frightened to move, and I'm not sure it's safe to do so, even if I weren't scared out of my damn mind.

At the feel of someone grabbing my arm, I gasp and my head snaps up, searching for the source. Maximus hauls me to my feet and half carries me until we're crouched behind one of the semitrucks. Through the strands of my hair, I watch him shoot and take cover, handling his weapon with a confidence I want to admire.

"Don't let that motherfucker escape!" His shout causes me to jump, but Maximus is too preoccupied to notice. "Stay here, Emilia."

He gives the order without looking at me, and then he's gone. I scoot over until I can peek around the vehicle's tail-lights. Bodies are scattered about, but none of them are my father, much to my disappointment. Maximus walks over to where Leone and some other man are holding my abductor between them. My husband speaks to him, and though his voice is so mild I almost can't make out his words, his body is rigid to the point he could be made of stone.

"You may not know me," Maximus says to Pascal, "but if you did, you'd understand how fucked you are right now." The knife in his hand catches the glow of the building's motion-sensor lights. and there's a gleam along the length of the blade. He lifts the man's head by placing the metal tip under his chin. "Now tell me, who ordered you to take my wife?"

When Pascal doesn't answer, Maximus grins. It's maniacal. Not once has he ever looked at me like that. If he did, I'd be tempted to snatch that knife from his hand and slit my wrists. I know with certainty there's no chance my abductor will live.

And good fucking riddance.

In a flash of movement, Maximus plunges the blade into Pascal's shoulder. The man's grunt of pain crescendos into a scream when my husband twists the knife ever so slowly. I clutch my chest in shock and morbid fascination.

"Did you really think you could put your hands on her?" Maximus asks. It's not really a question though. His tone is full of disbelief, not genuine curiosity. He yanks out the blade, the blood coating it, creating the illusion it's now black, and stabs Pascal in the opposite shoulder. "My wife is not to be touched or fucked by anyone except me. She is mine, and I will kill anyone who threatens her, but first I'll make them bleed. One drop of blood for every tear she shed, and one scream for every ounce of pain she felt."

I shudder when Maximus rotates the blade again. Pascal's cries echo down the street, and my stomach spasms with nausea. Dizziness assaults me, forcing me to sit on the rough ground and rest against the vehicle. I want justice more than anything, but I can't witness this brutality, even if I'm not against it happening. Pascal deserves to die, and so does my father, who's gone...

And one day the Silvestri family will finish what they started.

"Signora."

I blink up at Dante, who's offering me his hand.

"Come with me," he says. "Signore wouldn't want you to see this." After I accept his assistance, Dante helps me to my feet and steadies me when I sway precariously to the side. "Can you walk?"

"What?"

Once the screams die down long enough for me to hear him repeat the question, I shake my head. I'm not sure if I can walk without falling over. In answer, Dante lifts me into his arms. First he held me around the waist to make sure I didn't topple over and now I'm being carried away by him. I've never been touched so much by someone other than Maximus, and the comparison—although minor—shows that I still yearn for my husband.

"Dante," Maximus says, his voice like the crack of a bullwhip.

The enforcer stops and turns while my husband's long legs cross the space between us, his strides full of energy and purpose. As soon as he's close enough for me to make out his facial features and the droplets of blood on his clothing, I shrink in Dante's arms.

Maximus is going to fucking kill someone. Well, besides Pascal, and it's probably me, based on the way my husband is glaring at me. "What the fuck are you doing?" he asks.

The enforcer must not sense, or isn't worried about, the livid expression on Maximus's face. "She's unwell," Dante answers simply.

My husband's entire demeanor softens for a moment at hearing this bit of information. And then like a shooting star, it disappears. "Wait here."

He heads back to the group. "Look at me," Maximus says, now towering over Pascal. "Just know that your death will serve as a warning to anyone else who thinks they can steal from me and live."

I shut my eyes and turn into Dante's chest to shield myself. The gunshot is a very loud heralding of the Frenchman's death, but I find it gives me a feeling of closure. He'll never hurt me again.

If only that was the one person I had to worry about.

"Give her to me."

Dante transfers me to my husband, and I watch the exchange warily. Maximus all but crushes me to his chest with his gaze throwing daggers at his enforcer. Now that I know how comfortable Maximus is with a knife, it's a wonder Dante doesn't fall dead to the ground.

Maximus quickly speaks with someone named Vaughn, and I only absorb a portion of the exchange. I'm safer than I was, but now that I know what Maximus's plans for me are, I can't relax. I'm too busy stressing about what's going to become of me. I have no assets or money, but if I did, I'd escape as soon as an opportunity presented itself. However, it looks as though I'll have to wait until we return to the United States in order for me to steal enough valuables to pawn for money.

Until then I just have to survive.

Maximus deposits me onto the leather seat of the vehicle, and I automatically reach for the seat belt. My shaking hands make it nearly impossible for me to secure the locking mechanism, and my husband standing there watching certainly doesn't help matters.

"Fucking shit," I mutter, still fumbling with the metal clip.

"Stop."

Maximus's command causes me to instantly freeze. He reaches for the belt, and I retract my hands to avoid touching him. It was so difficult not to lean against him while he held me, to not take in his strength. The feeling of safety I once felt around him is a distant memory. Anyone who would admit their wife into an asylum for no just cause is beyond evil.

He's back to being a fallen angel, but he might end up being Lucifer to me.

With my seat belt fastened, Maximus enters the car for a long ride back to the hotel. Even the Paris lights do nothing to lift my spirits, though I'm desperate for an inkling of hope. However, even if I were to find some, I wouldn't trust my instincts. I actually thought Maximus was starting to see me as something more than a means to an end. He played his role so well I had no idea what his true intentions were for me.

But I'd be crazy to forget now.

The irony of that is my insanity's what pushed him to marry me in the first place. I guess it's best if I revert back to that and play the part.

Just like he did.

~

THE MOMENT we entered the hotel room and the door shut behind us with a clicking sound, Maximus's control threatened to crumble. I'm glad Otello was found unconscious, but his being alive didn't lessen the tension emitting from my husband.

I've been watching him with panic building in my chest for over twenty minutes, and the entire time he's paced back and forth while occasionally running his hands through his hair. I wait for the explosion that's coming, praying I make it out alive with my limited freedom still intact.

Maximus stops so suddenly it jolts me, and I rear back the second his gaze finds mine. The emotions within his dark eyes are too tumultuous to make sense of, and I'm not sure I should try, or if I even want to.

"Did...are you...fucking hell!" He runs a hand over his mouth and inhales deep, as though gearing up for something. "I've never been a smooth talker. That's Rafael's shit, but I can't get the fucking words out, never mind correctly."

I wait. Apprehension settles over me, and it's partially due to seeing Maximus unsure of himself. He's always in control, in command of his actions, and nothing is done out of emotion. Right now he's acting human, and it's different, out of character for him.

"Did they...touch you?" His voice is hoarse, a scratchy cotton instead of the silken tone I've grown accustomed to hearing.

I tilt my head. "Are you asking for me or for yourself?"

"Son of a bitch! Are you fucking with me right now?" He resumes his pacing, but it's faster now. "Jesus Christ and all the saints. You were abducted by the French mob, Emilia. For fuck's sake."

"I'm sorry if having a *used* wife isn't what you wanted," I say. He whips his head toward me as though I've slapped him. I squint at him, holding his stare, though it's intimidating. "But you knew from the beginning I was defective. It's part of your plan, to have me committed, so me being defiled and insane shouldn't matter to you."

The hurt and anger inside me heat until they're about to bubble over. I get to my feet with the intent to get away from Maximus. Just looking at him pains me, and the fact I wish he'd hold me infuriates me. He's a horrible person, yet the need for his comfort pulls me to him. Damn him and those moments of gentleness. They teased me, giving me dreams that turned into nightmares.

And I need to wake the fuck up.

My steps carry me to the door, powered by emotion. There's nothing logical about what I'm doing, but I don't care. I can't be around him for another minute, and the very thought of being in the same room, let alone sharing a bed, causes my insides to fume.

"Where do you think you're going?"

His voice is dangerous. It only serves to increase my speed. I grip the door handle and wrench it open, but it halts after a foot, the arc of the door coming to such a sudden stop it's jarring. Maximus grips the back of my neck, pinching my skin, and then curls his arm inward to swing me around to face him. I stare up at him in a stupor as he slides his hand to my throat right before slamming me into the door. The locks click into place, both for the door and for my chance at escape.

He brings his face close to mine, and his angry breaths brush my lips. "I said, where in the fuck do you think you're going?"

His hold on me isn't tight enough to where I can't speak, but I don't want to. The words hook themselves in my throat and dig into my tongue, eliciting a sharp pain. If I let them out, they'll only do more damage. Instead of parting my lips, I press them together.

"There's nowhere you can go that I won't find you." He runs this thumb up and down the side of my neck, and if he didn't look like he wanted to murder me, I'd mistake that touch for a caress. "You are my wife, and I will always come for you and bring you back."

Under different circumstances, his words would be considered romantic, loving even, but they're not. I steel my heart against them, reinforcing the walls he destroyed with temporary kindness.

"Now," he says, "tell me what I want to know. Did they rape you?"

I give a subtle shake of my head. This is a small acquiescence, and I allow it because Maximus is unstable right now. It's one thing to provoke him but another to engage in a battle where he'd crush me.

He surprises me by squeezing his eyes shut, his face a canvas that has streaks of both pain and relief. Then he drops his head into the curve of my neck, resting his forehead on my shoulder. "Thank fuck." His agonized whisper skims my collarbone, and my pulse races all the more. "I don't know what I would've done if..." He clenches the hand on my throat, and I hold my breath.

But when he grabs me between the legs, I let the breath out as a silent cry.

"This," he says, dipping his fingers into my panties, "is mine."

I'm drenched. This savage, feral side of Maximus excites me like nothing else. Maybe it's wrong or maybe it's acceptable, but that doesn't matter. I only care about what I want, and when he thrusts two fingers inside me, I groan.

"So fucking wet." He lifts his head to give me a licentious grin. "Say what you will, wife, but your cunt knows it's master. Now tell me where you were planning on going?"

As determined as I am to remain silent and keep Maximus from knowing my inner thoughts, I'm powerless against what he does to my body. He fucks me with his fingers until I'm sagging against the door, only held up by his hand on my throat. Pleasure overwhelms me, heightened by the raw emotions coming from both him and me. He's using my need for release to coerce me into giving him what he wants, and we've danced this dance before—him leading and me following.

Maximus repeats the question and accentuates each word with a tap to my clit. I'm panting, the streams of air short and cut off, but one carries a word. "Away."

He stops all movement. "Away where?"

Another single word, another nail in my coffin of vulnerability. "Anywhere."

"Don't play games with me."

"Anywhere you aren't," I grit out.

Can the universe stop spinning for a single moment? If that's a possibility, it happens right then and there. I glare at Maximus, letting my eyes convey everything I can't say. His gaze flashes with something that could be pain. Then it hardens, darkens.

"No." He shakes his head as if that will make his message clearer, more definitive. "Never."

A malignant current washes over me, originating from him. It paralyzes me, and I stand there helpless when he slams his mouth to mine. His lips are warm and soft, yet his kisses are anything but. He battles with me, conquering with every slant of his mouth and nip of his teeth. Then he claims me as soon as my lips part, his tongue sweeping into the cavern of my mouth. I grab handfuls of his shirt, thinking to shove Maximus, and instead I pull him to me. The anger rolling off us both only serves to career us into passion, leaving everything else behind.

My panties are torn from my body in his frenzy to have me bared to him. I'm lost in him, drinking in his domineering kisses and relishing the rough touches. At the feel of the head of his cock near my sex, I about weep, so desperate for connection, both physical and emotional.

Maximus is what I want, what I need, and what I should run from.

He grabs my hips and slides me along the door, looking up at me with such hunger it almost frightens me. *Almost.* I grip his shoulders and dig my nails into the solid muscle there, loving the feel of his strength and knowing it could be my downfall. Then I wrap my legs around his waist to bring him close.

"I'm never letting you go," he says. His hands tremble against my skin, and I know it's not due to him straining under my weight. It's because he's holding something back. "You're my wife, Emilia, until death."

I moan when he joins us, burying his cock fully within me. My eyes flutter closed as he pistons into me with a brutal pace, and instinct tells me it's not to hurt me. He's driving out demons in his soul and using my body as a sanctuary, propelling me into a state of nirvana from the ecstasy he's giving me. Like a benediction, Maximus whispers my name and worships me with everything he has. His lips, teeth, tongue, hands, and cock—there's not a part of him that he doesn't offer in sacrifice with the need to please me. And he does.

"I'm coming," I say on a whimper.

"Yes, you're coming back to me."

I spiral into a void where there's nothing but Maximus and the bliss he gives. My cries are accompanied by his groans and unintelligible words that hold so much intensity and conviction. His cock swells in me, and my cries morph into screams as he joins me in the surrender of his body. Tremors course through him, and I experience every single one, knowing they're born from release but also emotion. Maximus can't express what he feels, and he doesn't have to. I can sense it as if his body is my own. And right now he's telling me so many things that I pray to God are true.

He lays his head on my chest, and I weave my fingers through his hair, wanting to maintain the intimacy with him for however long it lasts. I'm not ready to face reality just yet. Instead, I enjoy having him inside me, his heart beating rapidly against mine and his hands gripping me tight.

"My mother left when I was too young to remember anything except the smell of her hair and the sound of her laughter," he says quietly. "The Wolf Pack hunted her because of what Caruso accused her of, and to this day, I'm not sure if she's alive or not, but I've never stopped looking and hoping, despite getting this tattoo in her memory and having attended her funeral. And I've never forgotten how her absence destroyed my father. He was a formidable man, strong and certain of himself, but when she disappeared, he withered over time to become a ghost."

Maximus nuzzles my breast, and I stroke the nape of his neck, offering comfort however he'll let me. Eventually he continues. "That is what'd happen to me if you were to leave, which is why I'll kill those who threaten you, and protect you from those who'd harm you. But I can't do that if you're gone."

He lifts his head and pierces me with his gaze. "This is why you can never leave. Do you understand what I'm telling you?"

Maximus cares for me. Whether he knows it or not, *that* is what he's saying.

I cradle his face and nod once. The tension lining his body, and the creases in his face vanish. He takes a deep breath and releases it slowly, and I believe some of the darkness exits his soul in that moment. I doubt all of it will ever go away, and I've made my peace with that.

He can't move in the underworld without blending in with the shadows around him.

AN HOUR later I prop myself up and look down at Maximus, taking in his bare chest and slightly damp hair, courtesy of our shower earlier. But mostly, I stare at his onyx eyes. They are shining as though newly polished, and I'm drawn to them, to the tenderness in them.

"What is it?" he asks. His brows snap together, and his lips thin. "What aren't you telling me?"

He starts to rise, and I place my hand on his sternum to lightly stay him. "I want you to know I'm sorry for whatever my father did to you and your family. If…"

I feel like an idiot, but I'm desperate for him to know how much I care for him. Maximus told me in his way, so I need to find mine. Besides, I want to move past what's been done and be rid of my father's presence in my marriage, starting with the removal of that damn tracking device, which my husband swore he'd get out as soon as possible.

"If what?" Maximus prompts.

I swallow my nerves. "If there's anything I can do to help or to…I don't know, but whatever it is, I want you to know I'll be there."

He slowly nods, and the thoughts flickering over his face are too difficult for me to decipher. "What about what he did to you?"

"Me?" I blink at him. "I had to let go of that or it would've killed me. I'm still furious over my mother's murder, but there's nothing I can do." I bite my lip and give in to my impulse by cupping Maximus's jaw. "However, I have a husband who will get justice for me, and that's more than good enough."

He peels my hand away from his face, and I still, saddened that he seems put off by me touching him. Then he kisses my palm and laces his fingers with mine. His mouth tips up on one side, and my heart squeezes in my chest. "I guess I'll have to follow through so I don't disappoint," he says. "I didn't realize wives preferred revenge over flowers."

I press my lips together to keep from grinning like a fool. "Fact: Flowers are thought to elicit positive human emotion due to their sensory properties. However, I don't see the practicality in flowers because they die rather quickly."

"I can understand that," he says with a serious nod. "What gift would an extremely logical and practical woman want? A Glock?" The smile on Maximus's face widens, and his eyes shine.

A giggle escapes me, and then I clear my throat, resuming a stern expression. "Perhaps, but I think I'll take his vow instead." When he raises a dark brow, I continue. "Loyalty 'til death. My husband will always have mine."

My confession has been made: I love Maximus.

Before he rescued me from my abductor, I was certain Maximus was going to let me die. And after that I believed my husband was going to lock me away, but now I know differently. My husband explained how he had to say something my father would not only accept but believe as truth. It didn't take me long to forgive him.

Admitting my feelings for Maximus is one of the hardest, and most vulnerable, things I've ever done. And now I'm sick with nervousness. I close my eyes to help with the nausea coming over me. A rejection from him now will wound me, more than anything else that's happened between us.

At him wrapping his hand around the back of my neck, my eyes fly open. Maximus brings his face close to mine and whispers, "Loyalty 'til death, *Mrs.* Silvestri."

My lips are trembling when Maximus pulls me to him and kisses me.

A vow.

A title.

A commitment.

These are the greatest gifts I could ever want.

Logic and flowers be damned.

MAXIMUS

"*H*ello, Tristano," I greet while tucking my weapon into its holster.

"While you've been busy touring Paris, your brother has gotten engaged."

"Get the fuck out."

Tristano clears his throat in warning over the phone, but I ignore it. This is Rafael we're talking about, the brother who'd rather lose a finger than get married. "Who and why?" I ask.

"Carina Nardone, and as to the why? He said it's because she's offered to feed us information in exchange for the protection of the Silvestri name."

"Holy shit."

"Indeed," Tristano says. "I'm not sure if this plan of his is foolish or brilliant, but the fucker didn't ask me before he agreed. Typical of Rafael."

I grin and huff out a laugh. "True."

"When you return, we'll need to discuss the events that transpired in Paris." He's back to being the head of the family, and there are times when I wonder if Tristano ever relinquishes that role, even when no one is around. I don't envy the authority or the burden associated with it. "Since Caruso's in line for a seat on the council, it'll make him that much more powerful, ergo, harder to destroy. But maybe Rafael will be able to divest the Nardones of vital information during this farce of an engagement."

Tristano swears under his breath, and I can picture him scowling. "Regardless of all that, I'm relieved you and your wife are well," he says. "I wouldn't have arranged for you to meet up with Fontaine if I'd known how much risk would be involved."

"I know, and I wouldn't have brought Emilia with me either. We'll have to be more mindful in the future about these things."

"I can tell you care for her, Max. Don't bother denying it. I raised you and know you better than anyone. This woman has changed you."

A cross between irritation and anger spreads through my body. "What the fuck are you trying to say?"

His exhale is long and loud. "That I'm happy for you. And perhaps a little jealous."

My eyes go wide. Emilia's brow creases with concern, and she stops in the middle of putting on her coat. Then she tilts her head in question, and I give her a wink. Her lovely face goes back to glowing with happiness, and I bask in it. Looking at her, I completely understand what my brother is saying. Having her light in my life, that of my *ragazza solare*, is the thing I want most in the world. My revenge has transformed into a need for justice, to correct the past's wrongs, but it doesn't mean more to me than my wife.

Nothing will.

My voice softens, as it usually does when I speak about my wife. "She reminds me of our mother, Tristano. Emilia is joy and peace yet strength and courage. I understand our father a lot better now."

"Yes," my brother says slowly. From his tone, it's obvious to me he's thinking. When he speaks again, there are no traces of longing in his voice. "When are you coming home? It's not safe for you to be in the *Unione Corse*'s territory after killing one of their men who's higher up the chain of command."

"I've arranged for his death to remain concealed until we touch US soil. That'll give me enough time to do one final thing before we leave."

"Very well. Safe travels, brother."

"Thank you," I say. After I tuck my cell phone in my pocket, I face Emilia. "Ready?"

She nods. "Are you sure we have time for whatever we're doing?"

"I'm making the time."

A SHORT WHILE LATER, Emilia bites her lip and hesitantly meets my gaze only to look away. "Why are we here, Maximus?"

I gesture to the love lock bridge with a small sweep of my arm. "I ruined your last experience here, and I want to replace that memory with a different one, a better one."

She gives me one of her smiles, and the urge to kiss her rises. "I have other memories," she says.

"It's not good enough." I slide my arm around her waist and tug her so that our bodies are flush. Her curves press up against me, and that has me counting down the minutes until I can get her alone. "Hold out your hand," I say, digging into my pocket. Once she does as I've instructed, I place the item on her palm.

Emilia's eyes fill with tears the second she opens them, and guilt rears its head. I'm such a stupid asshole.

"This was a fucking terrible idea," I mutter. Which a scowl, I reach for the gift, and she closes her fingers around it. "Give it to me."

She shakes her head, compounding my confusion. "Maximus, I love this."

I can't help my expression of skepticism. "Then why the hell are you crying? You rarely do that."

"I'm so touched you'd do this for me."

Emilia sniffs daintily but doesn't wipe her face. So I sweep my thumb across her damp cheeks. Her skin is blotchy from her tears, but she's still beautiful. She gazes down at the shiny gold lock in her palm, the one engraved with her and her mother's names. I hoped it would be a peace offering between her and me, to smooth over my past history with her. But if she's acting like this with the lock, I'm not sure I should give her the other present.

She gets up on her toes and brushes her soft lips against mine. "Thank you. This means so much to me." Her voice gets choked up again, and she clears her throat. "This memory is one of the best in my life."

I give her a tight nod, still uncertain if I made the right choice. Emilia pulls away from me and stares at the bridge for a long time, and after several minutes, I contemplate whether I should help her. But finally she chooses a spot, and there's a tiny click as she secures the lock. I walk over to her and rest my hand on the small of her back, offering my support with something other than words.

Emilia looks down at the key lying on her palm, and she whispers to it, telling her mother all the things she's kept hidden inside her. That's when I learn Emilia's mother was murdered by Caruso because she tried to help two trafficked girls escape. My wife continues speaking, revealing personal thoughts and feelings I had no clue about, and eventually kisses the small piece of metal.

She tosses the key into the river and turns to face me, tears running down her cheeks again. I tighten my hold on her and use my free hand to tilt up her chin.

"That was...cathartic." She inhales a shaky breath. "And I finally feel as if I have closure over her death. Thank you." Emilia gives me a watery smile.

I lower my head as well as the volume of my voice. "You won't thank me when I spank your ass raw for lying to me. You speak Italian, and from what I heard during your conversation with your mother, *fluently*."

Emilia's face blossoms with red. "And French."

"No more secrets," I growl.

She disarms me with a kiss. "*Oui.*"

I blow out a breath that's partially a laugh, and with it goes my irritation. "Well, fuck it. I might as well make you cry some more." My wife stiffens in my hold until she sees the object between my thumb and index finger. Tears well in her eyes, and I inwardly groan. "I fucking knew it."

Emilia silently cries while I slide the diamond band onto her ring finger. "Stop that," I snap. She grins at me and shakes her head. Her defiance turns me on like nothing else. "You're definitely getting the belt," I say with a firm nod. "No question."

Her breath hitches, and her cheeks redden further. "Promise?"

"Fuck me."

"Okay."

I take her hand and all but drag her to the car with her laughter ringing out.

My wife's name means "rival," and that's exactly what she was to me—someone I was in opposition to. Our marriage began on a battlefield, and I knew I'd be victorious because my name translates to "greatest." And I won, but it wasn't in the way I thought.

Instead of her pain, I won her heart.

Instead of her sadness, I won her laughter.

Instead of her death, I won her ability to bring me back to life.

Husband and wife, "greatest rival"—she and I against the world.

I THEE LUST

CARINA

The sound of the gunshot explodes in my ears.

It's followed by a deafening silence, yet does nothing to suppress the pounding of my heart. Time slows, as is often described by others, and my mind separates from the situation, giving me a view as though I'm seeing everything through a camera lens.

However, this filter offers no protection, only clarity in those few seconds.

The reward must outweigh the risk.

The cause must explain the effect.

In my case, the reward is life, with the risk being death. And the cause of all this violence? Treachery that begets suffering, the effects of which has my soul wailing and darkening.

A strangled cry, dislodged from me by terror, is lost in the cold wind. But a scream builds in my chest when Frederico's body folds in on itself and drops to the pavement, his lifeless gaze staring up at nothing.

The perpetrator aims his pistol in my direction and our gazes lock; Mine full of disbelief and horror, his overrun with bloodlust that shifts into a pure lust. If it can be considered such a thing?

"Hey, pretty lady," he says. The scratchiness of his voice scrapes along my skin and it prickles with fear, as well as disgust. "I saved you from this drug dealer, so you don't need to be scared of me."

The hitman takes a step toward me and I match it by retreating, maintaining the small distance between us. It's still not enough. He runs his gaze over me, too thoroughly. Then glint in his eyes is followed by his brows snapping together.

It's my only warning.

He's on me before I can draw breath. This forceful contact activates my sense of time and everything careens into a fast pace, the present no longer in slow-motion. My spine hits the brick wall when he slams his body into me and the acrid smell of gunpowder assaults my senses the moment he presses the barrel of his gun into the side of my neck. Warmth, from both the metal and his hand on my throat, seeps into my skin and my pulse ratchets up in protest. My lungs burn with a repressed shout.

The man leans in and places his foul mouth close to my ear. "You can't run from me and if you do, I'm going to fuck you all the harder because of it. You must like getting fucked by *made men*, so I'm here to finish what that rat started."

The reward of life outweighs death.

But in my estimation, the risk of death outweighs assault.

Adrenaline surges within me, speeding through every nerve ending I possess, and shocks me in motion when the stranger grabs my thigh and shoves his hand up my dress.

The time for analytical thinking is over, and has been since the minute I witnessed his gaze flash with dark intent.

My pistol is revealed with a sharp flick of my wrist. Which the man would notice if he wasn't tearing at my clothes. Sordid images flood every crevice of my mind and my past rears its ugly head, paralyzing me.

Unwanted touch.

Unwanted proximity.

Unwanted nightmares.

This can't happen again. I won't let it, no matter the cost.

I squeeze the trigger. The recoil causes my hand to jerk, but I don't stop, firing again and again until a clicking sound notifies me that my only source of defense is null and void.

The risk has now amplified.

My gaze collides with the stranger's and in that moment we are the only people in the city, or in the world. I stand there with my eyes wide, my erratic breathing pushing air past my parted lips, and watch his gaze flare with revelation as his hands fall away; One from my the juncture between my thighs and the other from my throat.

He looks down at his chest, then at the weapon in my grasp, still pointed at him, and finally brings his focus to me. His mouth, already slightly agape, attempts to produce sound without success. And then his gun hits the pavement, right before his body joins it.

A nearby shout snaps me out of the haze of death surrounding me. With one hand still gripping my pistol, I retrieve my phone from my purse and take a picture of the man who threatened me.

Then I drop to a crouch and pat down his lifeless form until I come across his personal effects. After snatching up his phone and wallet, I move to do the same to Frederico. A sickening guilt swamps me and I almost vomit my dinner; the one he paid for less than twenty minutes ago.

I push past the nausea to locate Frederico's belongings, and right when I go to grab them I hesitate. A million thoughts race through my mind, compounding my guilt and turning it into an almost living entity. It wraps around me like a shawl woven with threads of death and deceit. The sensation weighs on me and my outstretched hand struggles to stay airborne.

I lower my arm and do something stupid. With my eyes closed, leaving myself vulnerable to anyone approaching, I rifle through Frederico's pocket and retrieve the contents inside. I lift my heavy eyelids and stare at his body through my cell phone's camera lens but only briefly.

The small click frees me to leave, somehow thrusting me a little more into reality.

At the faint whining of a siren, I stumble when I get to my feet, and only the shaking of my legs keeps me from bolting. After peeking around the corner to verify no one has seen me, I boldly stride across the sidewalk. My gait becomes more steady with each step and by the time I reach the curb, I believe I appear calm to anyone passing by.

Once I hail a ride share, I tap my foot incessantly. A normal person would interpret my repetitive action as impatience, but what they don't know is I need an outlet for the emotions roiling through me. They're growing exponentially with intensity and I've repressed them as much as I can. My body still battles to keep tumultuous energy contained.

I'm a ball of molecules with increasing movement and if I don't have release, I'll implode.

My transportation pulls up to where I stand, and I all but jump into the waiting vehicle. The driver, a man in his late thirties eyes me warily, and I don't blame him.

I did just leave a crime scene where I murdered someone.

"Where do you want to go?" he asks.

"Anywhere but here."

He opens his mouth and promptly closes it. Then says, "Sounds good."

The car rolling away from the sidewalk and into traffic eases my anxiety somewhat. The Chicago lights are bright and lively, completely opposite of the dread and darkness swirling within me, within my soul, made darker by the latest events.

Thoughts of the lifeless bodies I left behind stab at my consciousness and I wince from the guilt of them. However, I shove all that line of thinking to the recess of my mind until I can handle it.

I can fall apart later, but my priority right now is to find safety.

How can I do that when this entire city is full of people with evil dictating their behavior? I'm in a web of my own-making, due to my actions, but I wouldn't be if not for my heritage. And who can fully escape their past?

Physically it's possible, but mentally there's nowhere to run.

Chills skid along my arms and I grab the ends of Frederico's jacket, pulling them closed. Not too long ago the wind soothed my flushed face, while the ends of my hair danced about my head. Not too long ago Frederico was my greatest, immediate threat.

But now he's dead and another, deadlier, threat has taken his place.

"You don't need to escort me home," I say to Frederico.

"The heart of the city is no place for you to be alone, especially at night." He glances down the street, no doubt searching for the ride share he requested on my behalf. "Why don't we get out of the elements while we wait?"

"You're right. It's freezing," I say.

He dips his head in acknowledgment and frowns. "Do you want my coat?" He shrugs from the long overcoat and holds it out to me.

"Please keep it." I gaze up at him a give him what I hope is a grateful smile. "I'm sure the driver will be here any minute, so there's no need for you to be cold."

He removes the garment and places it over my shoulders, and I have to press my lips together to keep from cringing. The entire evening has been this way: Frederico executing light touches and me trying to avoid them, or hide my disgusted reaction when he's successful.

To be fair, I don't want anyone's hands on me ever again.

"I'll be fine." He pulls out his phone from his pocket and glances at the illuminated screen. "It won't be much long—"

The cocking of a gun cuts off Frederico's words, as well as the air in my lungs...

I yank myself from the recent memory and massage my now throbbing temples. Has there ever been time when I wasn't under a constant threat of violence? The answer quickly arrives at the forefront of my mind.

No. I've never been safe.

The danger that began with my father still lingers, but it could originate from anyone in the crime syndicate, also known as the "underworld." The rulers of this corrupt kingdom delight themselves in putting others in tyranny.

Especially women.

And the probability of finding a white knight to save me? Laughable. Ridiculous.

However...

I can think of one *dark* knight who might protect me. Although he might not remember me. But I've never forgotten him, no matter how much I've tried.

"Equality and justice are not given to the faint of heart."

His words were delivered with a voice made up of temptation and secrets that still haunt me after two years. Could he be the one person to help me escape? Or will he be the one to lock me up in a tower, rendering me incapable from getting the thing I want most?

Freedom.

"Excuse me?" I say, my voice cracking. I clear my throat, and by that time the driver's gaze is on me in the rearview mirror. "I have an address now."

239

He nods after I tell him and then turns his attention back to the road, for which I'm grateful. The rest of the ride is silent, if I don't consider the screaming in my head. The nervous energy within me makes my skull pound and I massage my temples again, allowing the plan formulating in my mind to take shape. It's idiotic, reckless, and has the potential to get me into more dire straits than I'm currently in.

In this case, the risk outweighs everything, rendering the reward minute and the effect to be determined.

After a time I'm standing in front of the building that my dark knight calls home. It's a monolith of a building and I have no doubt he's claimed the penthouse as his place of residence. Rafael Silvestri may not be the head of his family, but he's the concierge, and that position of power will make him not only feel entitled but *be* entitled.

In a way, I guess the same could be said about me.

My inhale is long and deep as I mentally prepare for what's to come. I'm taking a gamble just by being in this part of the city where I could be identified by my father's men or anyone else who's aware of his seat on the Wolf Pack's council. And that's assuming Rafael doesn't notify my father of my whereabouts.

With that horrific thought in mind, I step up to the glass doors and thank the doorman when I walk over the threshold. The opulence inside is nothing I'm not used to and the beauty of it is lost on me, due to my growing apprehension. As inconspicuous as possible, I attempt to tame my wind-blown hair and smooth out the wrinkles in my dress. Rafael is a man, and similar to the other members of the criminal class, he'll be more likely to receive me if I'm presentable. Because that's probably all he believes a woman is good for.

If he only knew the things I've done…and would do again.

The thundering of my heart is louder to me than the clicking of my heels against the marble tile, and by the time I reach the front desk I'm rethinking my entire plan. The only thought that brings me the fortitude to continue is: *Rafael protected me once, so he might do it again.*

If not? Then I'll no longer be a damsel in distress but simply damned, awaiting the appearance of the next enforcer who will try to kill me. Until I can free myself of all this, I'm stuck in this purgatory.

But when in hell, dance with the devil.

I THEE LUST

RAFAEL

"*Y*our place is nice."

I nod at the woman running her manicured fingernails along the arm of my couch, and take a healthy swig of the contents in my tumbler. "Yes, it is. Now be a good girl and sit over here with me."

"I'd love to," she purrs.

Sara—at least I think that's her name—slinks over to me on six-inch heels, along with bright eyes, full of intent and cunning. Until I point to the space between my wide-spread legs.

She purses her fuchsia-colored lips in a pout that's supposed to be enticing, but I find it irritating. I should have lipstick stains on my cock already and all she wants to do is take a mental inventory of the items in my home, as if she's imagining herself living here.

Sandy has another fucking thing coming.

Well, *I* should be *coming*. But after I come in her mouth, and in her overeager cunt, she'll be gone. Like all the others before her. I prefer to fuck women in my house for many reasons, and the most important one being that it's heavily guarded.

The second is so I can tell them to leave.

I don't hold anything against these women for wanting a good time, since that's what I have them around for. But under no circumstances will they be allowed to stay the night.

They may have a pussy, but I don't take in strays.

Samantha stands before me and stares at me. I return the look and then flick my gaze to my cock. The hungry gleam in her eyes returns and she drops to her knees in between my legs. She's most likely envisioning pleasing me enough so I'll think she's special or worth keeping around.

Un-fucking-likely.

"So how do you want it, daddy?" She places her palms on my thighs and runs them upward until her thumbs brush my groin. "Do you want me to take it slow and drive you crazy? Or fast and put you out of your misery?"

"Lady's choice." I give her a wink in encouragement and she reaches for my belt.

About fucking time.

There are no formal rules when it comes to sucking dick, but I'm pretty sure it's frowned upon to shove a woman's mouth onto your cock until she can't breathe, let alone speak. It may be rude, but it's effective in getting someone to stop talking incessantly.

And it feels good. So, that's my go-to.

Samara pulls my belt, slowly with great theatrics, and then tosses it over her shoulder. I take another drink and wait for the show to be over. I've got things to do, people to kill.

The glamorous life of a *made man*.

As soon as my pants are unbuttoned and my zipper lowered, she slides her hand down my abdomen while making noises of appreciation. I down another swallow of alcohol and set my tumbler on the end table just as she wraps her fingers around my cock. Looking up at me, with her lashes flutter-ing, she lowers her head.

The ringing of my cell phone has me pressing my index finger against Suzie's lips. "One second."

She gives a playful huff and sits back on her haunches as I lean over to retrieve the phone. I frown at the screen, wondering why the employee who mans the desk downstairs is contacting me.

I press the answer button. "Hello?"

"Mr. Silvestri, I'm sorry to disturb you, sir. However, there's someone here that's requesting access to your floor and I wanted to notify you."

"Who is it, Mike?"

The guy clears his throat and that small hesitation piques my interest. "She doesn't wish to say, sir."

My brows draw together and I mentally sift through the women I know who'd act in such a secretive way. When I come up blank, I find myself intrigued. "I'm not going to allow this woman entry if she doesn't identify herself. You can tell her to cut the bullshit."

Sasha glares at me from her lowered lashes and I ignore her.

"He wants to know your name, miss," Mike says, his voice some distance from the phone. A soft, feminine voice flits over the line, but not enough for me to recognize the speaker. However, I find myself mentally trying to place the melodic cadence. "Sir, she wishes to speak with you."

My brows raise, despite me not having an audience; other than the blonde in front of me shooting daggers in my direction. "What do you think of her?" I ask Mike. He used to be a bouncer in one of the clubs I frequented and I hired him to evaluate and vet the people who enter this building. Not only because I live here and I own it, but due to his incredible memory and gut instincts.

"I would listen to what she has to say, sir."

"Very well. Put her on."

"Hello?" At the sultry voice gliding across my ear, I sit up straight. "Is this *Signor* Silvestri?"

"Yes," I say.

The unidentified woman releases a breath and it's full of relief. That's not the usual reaction I get from women. Most of the time they're panting from being fucked or huffing out of indignation. Just like Sage is right this minute.

I ignore her, giving this mysterious woman my full attention.

"It's Carina."

There's only one woman by that name in my psyche and she's the daughter of Paolo Nardone, a cold-hearted bastard who I'd love to see buried six feet under. Suspicion spreads over me, coating my mind and therefore, my words.

"What do you want?"

"Please let me speak with you," she says.

The desperation in her voice is far from artificial. If anything, the pitch and warble to her tone indicates a high level of stress. I'd go so far as to say panic.

"I don't have to step one foot in your home, and you don't even need to allow me upstairs," Carina goes on to say. "If I could have a moment of your time in the foyer, I would be grateful. Please."

Maybe it's the way she says the word *please,* as though I'm the only person who can help her. That alone strokes my ego. Yet, there's more to it than that. I know the life she's been raised to walk in, which has taught her a lot about men in the underworld. Knowing her father, Carina is well versed in ways to speak, act and dress. This plea from her could very well stem from this unique education, but the way she spoke to me is too raw to be pretense.

"Give the phone to Mike," I say. Her sharp inhale reaches my ears and there's a lot of displeasure in that. Once my employee is back on the line, I say, "Let her upstairs."

"Yes, sir." Then to Carina Mike says, "He will see you, miss."

I almost hang up, but choose to listen to however she responds. My curiosity is beyond intrigued by her appearance, shrouded in secrecy.

"He will?" She gives a nervous laugh, and the delightful sound makes my cock twitch. "Oh, that's a relief. Thank you, Michael."

Mike, the man who isn't scared to take a bullet or go up against someone twice as large as his six foot three frame, makes a sound at the back of his throat. Carina is obviously affecting him as well. Hearing this formidable tank of a human flustered is astonishing. "Please select the top floor, Miss Carina. If you require assistance, I can help."

"No, thank you," comes the reply.

"Will you need anything else, sir?" Mike asks me.

"No, and thank you."

I hang up the cell phone and toss it onto the couch. Then I secure the fastenings of my pants and fix Stephanie with a pointed stare. "Thank you for your company this evening. Unfortunately, something has come up and I'll need you to leave."

The blonde isn't quite able to hide the anger that flits over her features before her mask settles into place. "I can wait. Maybe in your bedroom, until your visitor leaves?" There's a hopeful note at the end of her question.

Too hopeful.

I get to my feet. My height isn't as impressive as Mike's but I'm still a solid six feet, towering over this woman, even in her heels. "That won't be necessary. Let me see you to the door."

When we walk across my living room, I ignore her subtle hints at wanting to stay or the way she basically drags each step as if that will give me time to change my mind.

"When will I see you again?" Shioban asks, gazing up at with a pitiful expression. Once again she pouts her bright pink lips and I find myself pleased with the fact that same hue isn't staining my cock.

A knock on my door has both our heads on a swivel and I open it. Carina Nardone stands there with her eyes wide, her face pulled into tight lines and her clothing rumpled.

And she's fucking gorgeous.

I can't believe I forgot how beautiful she is. No wonder Mike was mentally tripping over himself. I won't do the same, but I can't fault the man.

Carina's gaze zips back and forth between me and the blonde. Something in Carina's eyes darkens the hazel into amber. Disappointment? Disgust?

"Oh, I'm sorry," she says, her voice tight. "I didn't realize you were entertaining. I'll try again in the morning."

Before she can turn around completely, I wave a hand in dismissal. The action stalls her. "My guest was just leaving." I glance at Stella and subtly jerk my chin. "Thank you for coming."

I inwardly grin at my choice of words. Neither one of us *came*. But when I look at Carina, it's not hard to envision fucking her and *coming* inside her.

Simone finally gets the message I've been sending her for the past several minutes and leaves. But not without running her gaze over Carina's appearance in blatant assessment. Looking down her nose at Carina, the blonde briskly exits my penthouse, leaving a trail of cloying perfume in her wake.

"Come inside," I say, motioning to the living room. "Make yourself comfortable."

Carina pauses. It's slight but unmistakable.

This is understandable. She doesn't know me, at least not much beyond my reputation and our single interaction over two years ago. Yet, her hesitation surprises me since Carina is the one who contacted me. If she's having second thoughts, that's a sign. Of what, I'm not sure.

She gives me a tight nod and walks past me with her gaze level and her chin lifted. The scent of her, gardenia softened by a vanilla or something close to that, wafts under my nose. Instead of being sickly sweet or overpowering, the pleasant smell has me inhaling deep.

It's the same as when I met her but enticing nonetheless.

I rake my gaze over her sapphire dress and the brown coat that clearly belongs to a man. Her tawny hair that swishes back and forth with her confident steps. Whatever trepidation she felt earlier is gone.

Or she hides it well.

And who's fucking jacket is she wearing?

With my brows drawn, I turn and shut the door, making so that it's securely locked before facing her. Her clothing, although still flattering on her, isn't the quality I'd expect from someone of her status as the daughter of a boss. And her appearance? Yes, Carina obviously takes care to be presentable, but it lacks the over the top perfectionism I'm used to seeing from women like her. Normally, there wouldn't be a hair out of place, a smudge of mascara under her eyes, or her pretty mouth naked without some dab of color.

Carina is disheveled. No less of a beauty, but something is fucking wrong.

"Have a seat," I say, gesturing to the couch.

She settles herself on the chair, right next to the place I suggested.

A power move?

I walk over to the side bar and remove one of the crystal decanters from the stained-glass covered cabinets, as well as another tumbler. From my peripheral, I catch Carina open her mouth to refute the drink as I pour it, but she ends up pressing her lips together.

I hand it to her and she takes it, careful to avoid contact with me. "Thank you," she says. Carina sets the beverage in her lap with her fingers laced and her gaze honed on me. She waits until I sit across from her on the couch to speak. "I also want to thank you for agreeing to see me, *signore*. I wouldn't have interrupted you if I known about your..."

Her voice trails off and this should be the point I pick up where she left off, but I let her mentally flounder instead. The last time I saw this woman, she was openly defying her father right in the middle of the annual gala, made mandatory by the Wolf Pack; The council of the crime syndicate in which her father has a prominent seat. He is not someone to fuck with.

But then again, neither am I.

Carina was eighteen then and even as a new adult, she was formidable. I want to see if the last two years has strengthened her or if she's finally submitted to the will of someone. The owner of the coat, perhaps?

After a quick glance at her naked ring finger, I confirm it won't be that of a husband. This should've been the first thing I checked at her entering my home. No man approves of their wife visiting another man in the middle of the night at his residence. And one who's a *made man*? Well, that's just asking for people to get fucking killed. I like living my life too much to get offed by a jealous husband or fiance.

Not even for a chance to get between Carina's supple thighs.

Although, she is lovely enough for me to forget myself. That is a problem in and of itself. Maybe I need to test my resistance against her, as opposed to sussing out her resilience.

Carina daintily clears her throat and the hint of a blush taints her cheeks. "I didn't know you were preoccupied, is what I meant to say."

With my glass now full, I take a sip and nod. Again, I wait for her to lead the conversation, instead of asking her to appease my growing curiosity. She came here for a reason and I won't coax it from her. Unless she changes her mind. Then I might have to force it from her. That idea has my mouth tilting on one side.

And my cock hardening.

I swear to fuck that part of my body is the most impudent. But also, the most on point. It wants what it wants and when I look at Nardone's daughter, I can't act as if I don't understand why.

I like to own and fuck beautiful things.

"My company is gone," I say, "so you needn't be concerned with that."

Carina drops her gaze and stares at her lap, her index finger rapidly tapping the glass. While she gathers herself, I take in the delicate contours of her face, running my gaze along her arched brows, high cheekbones, and full lips. That damn coat conceals her figure, but her shapely legs, firmly pressed together, are visible since her dress stops at the knees.

When she snaps up her head and pins me with her gaze, now golden with whatever emotion is coursing through her, I take a sip of my drink.

"*Signore*," she says, her tone full of resolve, "I've come to ask you to marry me."

SERIES

Dark & Dirty Vows

A Match Made in Hatred
I Thee Lust
To Have & to Hurt

ABOUT AUTHOR

MORGAN BRIDGES

A lover of anti-heroes, deep and thought provoking books with beautifully written words, romance that's sigh-worthy, bedroom scenes that are so hot she blushes, and heroines that inspire her to the point Morgan wants to be like them when she grows up. Or she wants to punch them in the face and take their place in the hero's bed...erm...arms. Yes, that's it.

You can reach her at:

authormbridges@gmail.com